SORCERER

Regis P. Sheehan

First Edition Design Publishing
Sarasota, Florida USA

Sorcerer

ISBN 978-1506-915-54-8 PBK
ISBN 978-1506-915-55-5 EBK

November 2025

Published and Distributed by
First Edition Design Publishing, Inc.
P.O. Box 17646, Sarasota, FL 34276-3217
www.firsteditiondesignpublishing.com

This is a work of fiction. Names, characters, businesses, places, events and incidents are either the products of the author's imagination or used in a fictitious manner. Any resemblance to actual persons, living or dead, or actual events is purely coincidental.

The views expressed are those of the author and do not necessarily reflect those of the US Department of State or of the US Government

To the oppressed people of Iran.
May they soon see a better future.

"Like the dead in their coffins..."

~ Other Novels/Novelas by the Author ~

SUPPLICANT
The run-up to the 9/11 attacks of 2001 -

SICARIO
The hunt for Pablo Escobar in Colombia -

SURROGATE
Narco-Terrorism in the Caribbean -

SUCCUBUS
A North Korean diplomat attempts to defect to the West –

BLACK ENTRY
Covert CIA operations against North Vietnam -

www.**Sheehan-Fiction**.com

- Acknowledgments -

Associated Press - "Iran Confirms Processing of Tons of Uranium Ore", New York Times, May 10, 2005

Cale, Paul - "The United States Military Advisory Group in El Salvador, 1979-1992", US Army Command and Staff College, 1996

Cohen, Assaf - "The Fall of Heaven" The Pahlavis and the Final Days of Imperial Iran", Henry Holt and Company, 2016

Barbosa, Adriano M. – "Combating Terrorism in the Brazilian Tri-Border Area: A Necessary Law Enforcement Strategic Approach", Naval Postgraduate School, Monterey, California, June 2007

Bergman, Ronen - "The Secret War with Iran", Simon and Schuster, September 2008

Berman, Ilan - "Iran's Deadly Ambition: The Islamic Republic's Quest for Global Power", Encounter Books, December 6, 2016

Byman, Daniel - Chubur, Shahran - Ehteshami, Anoushiravan - Green, Jerrold - "Iran's Security Policy in the Post-Revolutionary Era", RAND Corporation, Santa Monica, CA, 2001

Central Intelligence Agency/Inspector General's Report of Investigation - Information Available to CIA Regarding the 1985 Attack on US Marines in the Zona Rosa", (96-0043-IG), September 18, 1996 (Declassified)

Charles River Editors - "The Trail of Tears: The Forced Removal of the Five Civilized Tribes", (Kindle)

DCI Counterintelligence Center - "Why People Spy: A Project Slammer Report", Central Intelligence agency, January 1993 (Declassified)

Director of National Intelligence DNI.gov/nctc/groups/hizballah.html

Duheaume, Tony - "Analysis: Iran's Secret Service and the History of an Agency of Assassins", Al-Arabia Website, August 18, 2018

FBI - "Year of the Spy (1985)", https://www.fbi.gov/history/famous-cases/year-of-the-spy-1985

Federal Research Division - "Iran's Ministry of Intelligence and Security: A Profile", Library of Congress, December 2012

Federal Research Division - Terrorist and Organized Crime Groups in the Tri-Border Area TBA) of South America", Library of Congress, July 2003 (Revised December 2010)

Finger, John R. - "Cherokee Americans: The Eastern Band of Cherokees in the Twentieth Century", University of Nebraska Press, Lincoln, 1991

Freedman, Lawrence – "The Future of War: A History", Public Affairs, 2019

Human Rights Watch - "Like the Dead in their Coffins: Torture, Detention and the Crushing of Dissent in Iran", June 6, 2004

IranWire - https://iranwire.com/en/features/65310/

Kokinos, Anyssia, Jahabani, Kanissa and Lewis, Jon - "Hezbollah's Operations and Networks in the United States: Two Decades in Review", Program on Extremism at George Washington University, Washington, DC, 2022

Levitt, Matthew – "Hezbollah Finances: Funding the Party of God", The Washington Institute, February 2005

Los Angeles Times - "KGB Reportedly Gave Arab Terrorists a Taste of Brutality to Free Diplomats", January 7, 1986

Offley, Ed - "Sources Finally Talk About 1985 Raid in El Salvador", Seattle Post-Intelligencer, 1996

Ostovar, Afshon - "Vanguard of the Revolution: Religion, Politics, and Iran's Revolutionary Guards", Oxford University Press, March 3, 2016

Perdue, Theda and Green, Michael D. - "The Cherokee Nation and the Trail of Tears", The Penguin Library of American Indian History, 2007

Pincus, Walter - "US Planned Retaliation on Salvadorans", Washington Post, January 18, 1997

Polmar, Norman and Allen, Thomas - "The Decade of the Spy", US Naval Institute Proceedings, Volume 115, May 1989

Rohter, Larry - "South America Region Under Watch for Signs of Terrorists", New York Times, December 15, 2002

Rose, Sunniva – "Shebaa Farms: Why Hezbollah Uses Israel's Occupation of a Tiny Strip of Land to Justify its Arsenal", The National, May 6, 2019

Smith, Michael - "Killer Elite: The Inside Story of America's Most Secret Special Operations team", Amazon Digital Services, LLC, December 11, 2016

Smith, Michael - "The Real Special Relationship: The True Story of How the British and US Secret Services Work Together" Simon & Schuster, 2022

Stratfor - "Special Series: Iranian Intelligence and Regime Preservation", June 22, 2010

Swanson, Doug J. – "Cult of Glory: The Bold and Brutal History of the Texas Rangers", Viking, 2020

Trevisi, A. F. - "Assessing the Terrorist Threat in the Tri-Border Area of Brazil, Paraguay and Argentina", International Institute for Counter-Terrorism, October 2013

US Department of State - "Patterns of Global Terrorism", April 30, 2001

Vogell, Heather – "Why Aren't Hedge Funds Required to Fight Money Laundering?", ProPublica, January 23, 2019

Wege, Anthony Carl - "Hizballah's Counterintelligence Apparatus", The International Journal of Intelligence and Counterintelligence, Routledge, Volume 25, Number 4, August 29, 2012

Wege, Anthony Carl - "Iran's Intelligence Establishment", The Intelligencer (Association of Former Intelligence Officers), Summer 2015

Wilder, Ursula M. - "The Psychology of Espionage", Studies in Intelligence, Volume 61 Number 2, June 2017, Central Intelligence Agency (Unclassified)

Contents

GLOSSARY OF ACRONYMS

ASAC - Assistant Special Agent in Charge
ATF - Bureau of Alcohol, Tobacco, and Firearms
AUSA - Assistant United States Attorney
CIA - Central Intelligence Agency
CHS - Controlled Human Source (informant)
CIL - Criminal Investigations Liaison (DSS)
DAO - Defense Attaché Office
DIA - Defense Intelligence Agency
DoS - Department of State
DS/DSS - Diplomatic Security/Diplomatic Security Service (US Department of State)
EDVA- Eastern District of Virginia (US Department of Justice)
FAM- Foreign Affairs Manual
FBI - Federal Bureau of Investigation
FMLN - Farabundo Marti National Liberation Front (El Salvador)
GTA - Global Threat Analysis (JICSA cover name)
IRGC - Islamic Revolutionary Guard Corps (Iran)
ISA - Intelligence Support Activity (US Army)
ISI - Inter-Services Intelligence (Pakistan)
ITA - Intelligence and Threat Analysis (DSS)
JICSA - Joint Interdepartmental Committee on Special Activities (The Org)
KGB - Committee for State Security (USSR, Armenia, other former Soviet states)
Legat - Legal Attaché' - FBI Representative at a US Embassy
LPR - Lawful Permanent Resident (Green Card Holder)
MOIS - Ministry of Intelligence and Security (Iran)
MSD - Mobile Security Division (DSS) (Now Office of Mobile Security Deployments)
NLETS - National Law Enforcement Telecommunications System

NSC - National Security Council
Org - The Organization (JICSA)
PNP - National Police of Paraguay
Post One - Visitor control point in a US Embassy/Consulate - manned by a Marine Security Guard (or MSG)
PRTC- Central American Revolutionary Party (El Salvador)
RFOA - Request For Assistance
RSO - Regional Security Officer
SA - Special Agent
SAC - Special Agent in Charge
SCIF - Sensitive Compartmented Information Facility
SIGINT - Signals Intelligence (communications intercepts)
SNSC - Supreme National Security Council (Iran)
SSG - Special Surveillance Group (FBI)
TBA - Tri-Border Area (South America)
TDY - Temporary Duty
UCMJ - Uniform Code of Military Justice
USCENTAF - US Central Command Air Forces
WFO - Washington Field Office

= ONE =

BORINQUEN

San Juan, Puerto Rico
May 21, 2004

"This music here is all shit," Escobar complained, dismissively waving a half-empty beer bottle about. "It's all like, uh you know, all ching-chukka-ching-chukka-ching... All the time. All shit."

Despite his nickname, though it was actually a war name, Escobar had not a drop of Latin blood in his Balkan veins.

"As if Bosnian music was any better," Chalice countered, grabbing a handful of popcorn from a shared basket. "Besides, I think what you're hearing is called *merengue*. It's Dominican. Like that beer you're drinking. Not from here."

"Bosnian music is shit too," agreed the reedy, tin-eared Zlatko Piric. He snorted and pulled a fresh bottle of Presidente from the iced bucket on the table between them.

Zlatko and Escobar should know. Both were Bosnian Muslims. Both were hard-bitten veterans of the tripartite wars between the Muslims, the Christian Serbs, and the Croats that tore the former Yugoslavia to pieces in the mid-1990's.

Likewise, both were also proven, long-term operational agents of the Org. The Org was more formally known - to those select few in the know - as the Joint Interdepartmental Committee on Special Activities, or JICSA. A largely off -the books operation, JICSA was a US covert action agency under the oversight of the National Security Council (NSC).

Chalice was the Bosniaks' American case officer. He had initially encountered them several years ago. That occurred in 1995, as part of the rendition of a Serbian war criminal, named Bojan Garivlolic, from the wildlands of Bosnia. At that time and ever after, they had always proven themselves to be loyal and reliable Org assets.

The three men were sitting under a trellis outside of a neighborhood bar. It was a Friday evening in San Juan. The night air, while gradually cooling, was still heavy with humidity.

The team was in Puerto Rico to meet with someone who was believed to be an official of Iran's Islamic Revolutionary Guard Corps - or the IRGC. Granted, Puerto Rico, also known as Borinquen as an historical salute to the Taino indigenous people who occupied the island prior to the arrival of the Spanish, was an odd place to meet a member of Iranian Intelligence. But that was where he was - so that was where they were.

"Dagger is coming in tomorrow?" Zlatko asked.

"On the morning flight from Miami," Chalice affirmed.

Dagger was a former member of the US Army's Delta Force and a relatively new member of the Org. The team had recent experience with him in an operation that had just concluded in Italy.

"And Dastan?" Zlatko continued. *Dastan*, which is how the man identified himself, was a Persian word that generally referred to the subject of oral histories. The Org was now using the term to characterize their current IRGC person of interest.

Chalice took a swig of beer and wiped his lips. "Plan is to meet him the day after tomorrow. Or even after that. You know how it goes."

"I know," Zlatko sighed dramatically. Truth be told, he was not that all unhappy to be passing the days on a sunny isle in the Caribbean. Nevertheless, with a flair of the dramatic he went on to add, "As some writer once said, *waiting is the rust of the soul.*"

"Who said?" Escobar demanded, in a tone as if offended.

"I don't know," Zlatko admitted "Someone."

"Glad you clarified that," Chalice observed quietly.

"And then after this... uh, rusting period. What then?" Escobar asked.

Chalice shrugged, idly swirling the beer in his own bottle. "And then we see what he wants... Dastan is essentially calling the play here. We have to engage with him to see what it is."

Prior to the 9/11 attacks, foreign intelligence collection was the province of the CIA and - if pushed - the DIA. After the al-Qaeda shock it was more or less unofficially determined that it was all hands on-deck. Whichever agency *could* help, especially in relation to counter-terrorism collection, *should* help. JICSA was happy to assist.

* * *

The next morning, the man they called Dastan finally made his wishes known. He advised that he would be available to meet that same weekend. His preference was for Sunday night engagement at a private house in a Santurce barrio.

Santurce was the most populous district on the island. Within its confines were the tourist and casino areas of the Condado.

Can do easy, Chalice replied in so many words. And it was so arranged.

Just prior to the meeting, the Org covering team, consisting of Zlatko, Escobar and the newly arrived man they called Dagger, moved into position near the house. There had been some discussion as to whether or not Chalice should go into the meeting wearing a ballistic vest.

On the one hand, it ran counter to normal agent recruitment operations. Establishing trust, rapport building and such.

On the other hand, this was the Iranians... Hence the armed covering team.

In the event, the final decision was that Chalice should go into the initial meet without body armor that could be visibly detectable and therefore detrimental toward developing a relationship with the Iranian officer.

However, he would be carrying a snub-nosed .38 caliber revolver in an ankle holster. And he would be wearing an emergency push-button alarm secreted on a wristband.

* * *

As the team was briefed, Dastan's preferred meeting point was a single -story private home on the eastern side of the Santurce barrio. It closely bordered a small lake called the Laguna los Corozos. In the distance across the water was the vibrant neighborhood of Isla Verde.

By pre-arrangement, Chalice waited until thirty minutes past midnight before he approached the door of the house. It was an older structure, a protest against the newer construction of the Laguna area. As planned, the door was ajar, inviting entry.

Even at that late hour on a Sunday, the muted sounds of music and celebrations could be heard in the distance. After running though his mental checklist, Chalice pushed the door open and stepped inside.

Moving though the gloom of the entry hallway, he belatedly wondered if the .38 should not have been in his hand, rather than affixed to a sheath on his ankle.

Chalice turned into the living room and there he was.

The man he knew as Dastan stood alone before him. He was a gaunt figure of medium height, in his early forties, forty-two years old, sporting a neatly shaped gray stubble of whiskers on his chin and cheeks.

Despite his genteel appearance, Chalice understood that his erstwhile host had been an early adherent of the Khomeini sect and was now a mid-level officer of Iran's Revolutionary Guard's Corps (IRGC). The IRGC was a rival of the formal MOIS intelligence service, the agency that specialized in western hemispheric operations.

"*Salaam*," Chalice said.

Dastan nodded. "You are Mister Greenway?"

"I am. Can I come in?"

"As you like," he said. "Enter."

Chalice quickly scoped out the living room as he entered. It was adequately furnished, but dreary in the extreme. Without personality. It had all the outward appearances of a sterile safe-house. It gave Chalice reason to wonder just how active the Iranians had been in Puerto Rico.

"Are we alone?" Chalice asked.

"Clearly." Dastan motioned to a coffee table that held two small ceramic pots and two cups. "Tea - even at this late hour?'

"Thank you."

They sat opposite each other as Dastan poured tea from the two pots. "And so," he said, indicating the cups with a flourish. "Cheers."

"Cheers," Chalice replied, taking a sip of the tea.

The Iranian took a sip of his own tea and replaced the cup in its saucer. "Thank you for agreeing to meet with me."

Chalice nodded. "You asked for this meeting... Why are we here?"

"You are with American Intelligence?"

"You could say that I am the proper channel for your questions," Chalice deflected.

"I hope that you are," Dastan said. "I have important information to convey to your government."

"Such as?"

"A way to benefit both of our nations. Information relating to Israel."

"Not to be indelicate," Chalice said. "But are we discussing a possible defection?"

"Not defection. Coordination."

Dastan chattered on aimlessly for several more minutes, stating his love for his country and need for better relations with the United States. However, the more Chalice gently prodded for specifics, the more abstruse Dastan's information became.

It was nothing that Dastan said - just something vibrating in the atmosphere that added to Chalice's growing discomfort. Folding his hands, Chalice unobtrusively pressed a concealed button on his wristband. By pre-arrangement, one push signaled the covering team to be alert. Multiple pushes sounded an emergency.

"I'm sorry. What?" he said.

"I said, have you ever been to my country?" Dastan repeated. "To Iran."

"Never," Chalice replied. He was conscious of a growing sense of light-headedness. Something in the tea?

"It is a beautiful country. Very historic. With a culture that is thousands of years old," Dastan crooned. "Many historic figures. Cyrus, Xerxes, Bardiya, Darius..."

"Thermopylae," Chalice interjected, emphasizing an ancient Persian defeat at the hands of the 300 Spartan Greeks.

"Well," Dastan said.

"This is all very interesting," Chalice said. "But not really germane to why we are here tonight... Why are we here tonight?"

Dastan studied him carefully. "We were thinking that maybe you should return to Iran with us."

"Us?"

His peripheral vison caught movement to Chalice's right. A large, sallow-faced man had emerged from an adjoining room. He was holding a pistol in his right hand.

"This is my associate, Turan," Dastan announced. "We believe that we can speak more freely back in my country."

Turan raised his gun, pointing it unwaveringly in Chalice's direction. Chalice pulsed the button on his wristband several times and rose to his feet. He was feeling a spike of adrenalin, despite the wooziness from the effects of the spiked tea. He slowly closed the distance between himself and the gunman.

A phrase from his Army combat training flashed through his mind - react to contact.

"I don't see the need for guns here," Chalice complained, starting to raise his hands submissively. "Or the need for travel. Maybe we..."

Suddenly, Chalice's left hand lashed out at Turan's gun hand. Instantly, he seized the length of the weapon, trapping it, and twisting it down and against the others body. As he did so, he stepped into Turan, punching him heavily in the face.

Taking a half-step back, Chalice twisted the gun out of Turan's hand with both of his, the action breaking Turan's trigger finger for good measure.

By now, Dastan was out of his chair, a revolver in hand. He fired twice, both bullets hitting Chalice in his left side.

Even as Dastan was firing, Escobar's squat form crashed into the room - button-holing to the left around the doorway. With his back to the wall, he also fired two times. The impact sent Dastan's body tumbling backward over the chair

Dagger was into the room a split second behind Escobar. A Kimber Custom .45 caliber was in a two-handed combat grip and aimed in on Turan's bulk. Without hesitation, he triple-tapped Turan, delivering two shots to the Iranian's chest and one to the head, just in case Turan was wearing body armor. He wasn't.

Zlatko was in behind them. He dropped to a knee to assess Chalice's injuries. It did not look good.

As Escobar and Dagger cleared the rest of the small house, finding it empty, Zlatko called 911 for medical assistance. He could hear the growl of an engine and the screeching of tires as a vehicle fled the scene from the rear of the house.

That done, he hit a speed dial to the 703 area code in Northern Virginia to signal an emergency.

= TWO =

QUASH

Washington, DC
May 22, 2004

Within the Org's command structure, there was, to put it mildly, no desire for publicity concerning to the incident in San Juan. Following the shooting, a slew of hurried calls traversed the miles between Puerto Rico, Northern Virginia, and the District.

Before dawn broke the following day, an official of the National Security Council was on the phone across town with FBI Headquarters, asking them to quash the shooting investigation on the island. The FBI duty agent acknowledged the request and quickly kicked it up to Management.

The Bureau's official reaction, in learning that a covert action agency was poaching on US territory - the Commonwealth of Puerto Rico - was one of annoyance. Nevertheless, after some internal grumbling, another call duly went out to the Special Agent in Charge of the FBI's San Juan Field Office in the Hato Rey federal office building. The SAC was equally displeased with developments, but he acknowledged his directions and reached out to the superintendent of the *Policia de Puerto Rico*.

Before lunch, the PR Police issued a routine press release through its media relations section. The statement announced that the multiple shooting incident that had taken place in Santurce was the result of a police undercover investigation into drugs and money laundering. Details to follow at some unspecified time in the future.

Noted. Follow-up questions deferred. And life went on.

* * *

Well before sun-up that morning Chalice had been taken to a local San Juan hospital for emergency treatment and stabilization. A few days later he was medically evacuated to the University of Alabama Hospital in Birmingham. UAB was one of several facilities with which the Org had contracted for just such unwanted developments. The other three team members, unscathed, came out on the same aircraft with him.

As the news of the incident filtered into the ranks of the Org, it was greeted with feelings of shock and dismay. These soon jelled into a cold desire for revenge.

= THREE =

IN DEFENSE OF THE REVOLUTION

Tehran, Iran

It can be said that the Iranian Revolution finally came of age in December of 1979. That was when the Ayatollah Ruhollah Khomeini, who had been exiled in Turkey, Iraq, and France for the previous fourteen years, officially became the Supreme Leader of the nation.

Aside from being the Supreme Leader, Khomeini also happily bore the title of "*Sayyid*" or "Lord." It was an honorific only given to descendants of the Prophet Mohammad.

After 2,500 years of kingly rule, the final iteration of a series of Persian royals - the Shahs of the Pahlavi family - were out of power. That occurred in December of that year when Shah Mohammad Reza Pahlavi, the *Shanhanshah*, or the King of Kings, finally fled the country for the last time.

The Shah had done so once previously. It happened before in 1953 - only to be restored by a joint CIA British SIS coup (Operation Ajax) - and then again in 1963 in the face of violent street demonstrations. He would initially find solace in America and then, at last, in Egypt.

Now the royal family was gone. The clerics, the sages of a hardline conservative brand of Shi'a Islam, were in.

A key entity of the new government was an entity known as the Supreme National Security Council (SNSC). Per Article 177 of the new Iranian Constitution, the role of the SNSC was three-fold: to develop national defense and security policies under the guidance of the Supreme Leader; to coordinate such polices with other organs of the state; and to confront internal and external threats to the country.

SAVAK, the Shah's former intelligence and security agency, was of course deemed passé (and worse). Its past members, now criminals, were regularly being hunted down and duly punished.

The theocratic regime, in turn, produced its own loyalist spy organizations to serve in defense of the Revolution. The Ministry of Intelligence and Security (MOIS) was formed in 1984 as the nation's primary foreign intelligence agency.

Unfortunately for the MOIS, the Islamic Revolutionary Guards Corps (IRGC) also known as the *Pasdaran*, and their subservient Quds Force, pre-dated them in 1979 and 1980. Those organizations remained as major contenders for power.

In March of 2004 a subsidiary arm of the IRGC called the *Basij* (a volunteer militia formally titled the Mobilization Resistance Force) demonstrated its loyalty to the regime in dramatic fashion. It aggressively responded to an International Women's Day demonstration in Laleh Park, Tehran. Armed with police batons, the Basiji violently attacked the demonstrators, many of whom were later arrested. Point made.

That same month a fundamentalist cleric named Hassan Rouhani was a senior staff member of the Supreme National Security Council as well as the deputy speaker of the Parliament. He was famed for saying that Iran would "not hesitate to crush the actions of groups abroad opposing the revolution." Nine years later Rouhani would go on to become the elected president of Iran. He would be reelected four years after that.

Hassan Rouhani knew whereof he spoke. The Islamic Republic had a rich tradition of seeking out and eliminating dissidents and others enemies outside of their borders.

Between 1979 and 1996 there would be at least ten well documented attacks by Iranian agents or their proxies beyond the borders of the Islamic Republic. These included shootings in Paris, Vienna, Berlin, and Bethesda (Maryland), stabbings in Switzerland and Japan, and bombings in the streets of Buenos Aires and in the skies of Panama. The nearly two decades of violence was capped with the truck bomb attack against the US Air Force quarters at Khobar Towers, in Dhahran, Saudi Arabia.

The resulting external body count to that point was, at minimum, 162 people killed and many hundreds more wounded and maimed.

And still counting.

= FOUR =

LANDAU

McLean, Virginia
May 28, 2004

The headquarters of the Org, more formally known among the cleared Beltway insiders as the Joint Interdepartmental Committee on Special Activities (JICSA), was located in a modernistic, yet aging building that occupied a space along the edge of the Washington Beltway. Boasting a yellow sandstone façade, it sat just off of Route 123 within the geographic limits of McLean, Virginia.

To the outside world, JICSA held itself to be a private risk assessment firm operating under the cover identity of Global Threat Analysis, or GTA. In its cover role, it was a commercial success. GTA's private sector clients were happy with the corporate intelligence services provided by its overt, legitimate side. In point of fact, GTA's insights into current political developments were highly regarded by its commercial customers who saw them as acutely perceptive and remarkably up to date.

In reality however, JICSA was a clandestine covert action agency that answered directly to the National Security Council. Structurally, it was comprised of a core professional staff that was liberally augmented with specialized contractors who served on an operationally as-needed basis. As a result, it was a flexible organization that could and did morph its structure to address its assigned missions as they arose.

* * *

An attractive, red-haired woman named Angela was patiently waiting in the SCIF, the building's Secure Compartmented Information Facility. It was the single secure room designated for discussions at the Top Secret level. As the location of a given SCIF in any building was itself classified information, the room was more commonly described among JICSA staff simply as Conference A.

Angela was preparing for a secure damage assessment meeting with the JICSA director, a retired one-star Army general - and former Delta Force commander - named JD Tucker.

A one-time hard targets analyst for the Defense Intelligence Agency, Angela was the Chief of Analysis for the Org. She and the JICSA director had a history, as it could be said. The less said about that - from her viewpoint, as well as Tucker's - the better.

Angela was not alone in the SCIF. Sitting across the table from her was a fit man of a certain age. Graying and balding, he was dressed in his usual work outfit: gray dress slacks, a white shirt with sleeves that were rolled to the forearms and a loosely knotted red tie.

A pair of reading glasses rested low on the bridge of his nose as he scanned a classified briefing folder on the table in front of him.

"You all set for this Bart?" Angela asked.

"As always," the other answered with a quick smile.

"*Semper Peratus,*" Angela mused. Always ready.

"Negative Angela," he responded. "That's Coast Guard stuff. I think what you mean is more like, uh, *Semper Fi.*"

Her sardonic subordinate's actual name was Bart Landau.

In his younger days, as an adventure-seeking college graduate with a liberal arts degree, Landau had enlisted as a private in the US Marine Corps. Happily bypassing a stint in the infantry, he wound up serving with an air wing in Okinawa, as an intelligence specialist.

Following that tour, Landau left the Marines to seek a career in the civilian world. He soon found one in the FBI. There he became a member of the SSG - or the Special Surveillance Group.

SSG members were normally unarmed, non-agent, full-time surveillance operatives. They typically spent a career between manning static observation posts and running operations on the street. The SSG actively tailed intelligence, terrorist, and criminal targets - all the while meticulously documenting their activities for further investigation or prosecution.

After a few years, the initial romance of SSG work began to deteriorate into a sense of day-to-day tedium. When that happened, Landau - unwilling to make yet another major career change - was able to transition from the SSG into a position as an intelligence analyst within the Bureau.

Drawing upon his military experience and training, he eventually became a recognized authority on the Iranian target.

Some twelve years into the job - and mindful of the old SSG lament that "there were two types of people in the FBI - agents and furniture" - he reluctantly left the Bureau to try his hand with a promising job in a little-known covert group across the river in McLean, Virginia. Somewhat to the disapproval of the FBI.

Nevertheless, as with the Bureau, Landau's specialty at the Org was focused on the threat presented by the Iranians and their Hezbollah adherents.

There was a whooshing sound as the heavy door of the SCIF was pulled open. "Greetings all," JD Tucker announced as he stepped in.

"JD," Angela said.

"General," Landau chimed in, nodding from his chair.

Tucker was followed by his deputy, Kurt Meyerhof, who pushed the door closed behind him and secured it. The deputy appeared to be in an uncharacteristically sour mood.

The only key figure who was missing - out for treatment of an old sports injury - was the man referred to as "ChiefOps", or Chief of Operations. ChiefOps was a newly designated position, created by Tucker, in response to the expanding role of the Org.

Tucker dropped into his regular chair at the head of the table. He smiled at Angela and nodded to Landau.

"Okay folks," he began, dispensing with introductory comments. "This is what we know for sure... A week ago, while trying to do a prospective agent meet down in Puerto Rico, Chalice and his team ran themselves into a fair shit storm. Chalice is down. The shooters themselves, two of them, are dead. The reminder of the team has been recovered."

"As you say, a fair shit storm," Angela agreed. "Undoubtedly."

"So, we know what happened but not necessarily who exactly was behind it." Tucker continued.

"A known unknown, as someone famously said," Meyerhof quipped.

Tucker nodded. "And I want to narrow down on that focus. I want to send some pay-back to the decision maker behind this. And pretty damn soon."

"As you know, JD," Meyerhof said, "the individual they were meeting with was calling himself Dastan. The first read from the Community is that he was an officer of the IRGC," referring to the Islamic Revolutionary Guard Corps of Iran.

"Well..." Landau interrupted.

"Well, what?" Meyerhof asked tightly, turning his attention down the length of the table.

"The Community has been wrong before," Landau said. "And I think they're doing it again."

"Meaning?" Tucker asked.

"The IRGC angle. It doesn't feel right to me."

"How so?"

Landau waggled his head almost imperceptibly as he organized his notes. "The IRGC - or the *Pasdaran* - is primarily a paramilitary group. An alternate military force in Iran. Protector of the Revolution. Supporter of terror groups, yes. But something like this... I dunno."

"Which is why..." Angela injected.

Landau nodded. "Which is why I think Dastan is MOIS, not IRGC," he said referring to Iran's Ministry of Intelligence and Security. "Also called VEVAK, in Farsi."

"MOIS is the more traditional intelligence service," Landau continued. "No military connection. But they are no slackers when it comes to aggressive actions overseas... For example, in the 1980's they established something in Lebanon reputedly called the Special Research Apparatus within Hezbollah. That was designed to execute their more valued operations against US and Israeli targets."

"Such as?"

Landau pushed his notes aside. "The MOIS has something called Department 15. Exporting the revolution is one of their imperatives. Department 15 seems to have a history of successfully chasing down dissenters abroad and killing them," he said. "Their most notorious action is the series of so-called Chain Murders that occurred between 1988 and 1998. Over eighty political activists were tracked down and killed during that decade."

"The worst single instance being in Armenia," Angela added.

"Why Armenia?" Tucker asked.

"It's believed that they staged a bus accident in a mountainous area of Armenia back in 1995," Landau said. "Bus went over a cliff. Twenty Iranian dissidents left dead."

"And so?"

Landau extracted a manila folder from a leather binder and opened it. "Yesterday I pinged an Iranian Affairs analyst that I know over at the Agency," he said. "I asked him to run the Dastan pseudonym through their databanks."

"And?" Meyerhof.

"Well, as you know, a lot of the Agency's foreign name checks are less than the hard biographical data that one would like. They're more representative of reports and chit-chat picked up from here and there."

"The point being?" Meyerhof prodded.

Peering at his report, Landau continued, "The Agency has a half dozen male figures in the databank referred to as "Dastan." The most promising one is a fellow with the possible true name of Ehsan Shahidi. Supposedly born in Esfahan, Iran, 1958 or thereabouts. Devout Shi'ite Muslim, as might be expected from an MOIS officer. Never married. Became an adherent of the Ayatollah Khomeini circa 1976."

Landau cleared his throat. "After the revolution, he joined the intelligence service at age 27 or so. Career officer. Last known assignment - Department 15 of MOIS."

"That's about as good as its going to get," Tucker opined.

"I agree," Angela said.

"So then, what were they up to in San Juan?" Tucker asked. "It's pretty far afield from their usual haunts."

Landau replaced his glasses to page though the file for a few more seconds of silence. Finding the exact page that he wanted, he continued, "Well, this Dastan fellow, now deceased... He apparently wanted to make contact with a US intelligence officer to, ah..."

"To defect," Meyerhof said, completing the thought for him.

"Not exactly, Meyer," Angela interjected, providing a bit of cover for Landau. "Our Dastan figure said that he was reaching out to the Americans to explore his options. Not precisely to defect. Not just yet anyhow."

"As in what kind of options?" Tucker asked.

Angela folded her arms and leaned onto the table. "I don't know if this has been briefed up to you yet, JD," she began, "but we do have a potential source right now in Iran. Someone who is still in the developmental stage."

As they all knew, *developmental* meant that the individual had been spotted as a potential source. That would have been followed by an assessment of his value as an agent. If deemed worth the effort, he would then be professionally massaged to see if he would be willing to step up into the role of being a real, honest-to-God spy.

Tucker turned to Meyerhof. "*Did* I know all that?" he asked.

"Probably in a briefing package a while back," the deputy replied with a frown.

"Okay. And the connection to all this with Chalice is... What?" Tucker continued.

"In his preliminary communications," Landau said, picking up the thread. "Dastan seemed to imply that he was aware of an American spy in the Iranian intelligence structure. We were interested in seeing if he was referring to our guy... Our developmental. Or if not ours - then whose?"

"Okay," Tucker agreed. "Go on."

Landau adjusted himself in his seat. "We're just making a supposition here," he said. "But what if Dastan's controllers have picked up the scent of an American agent in their ranks? And what if they wanted to send a cautionary message to his possible handler?"

"And hit Chalice by mistake," Angela said, concluding the thought.

"Maybe," Tucker mused. "Maybe we can leverage this."

"How so?" asked Meyerhof.

"The NSC," Tucker continued, "has been pushing to find ways to sting the Iranians. Disrupt their operational flow. Create uncertainty."

"Then," Meyerhof supplied, "we might be able to get some payback for Chalice while simultaneously hitting Tehran where it hurts."

"Quite possibly," Tucker said. "Quite possibly."

= FIVE =

QARANI STREET

Tehran, Iran
June 5, 2004

Shahriar Parviz came up out of the Taleghani subway station, appreciating a breath of fresh morning air. It was a Saturday, the first day of the work week; the Iranian version of Monday. Following a herd of his fellow work-a-day commuters, he began trudging down the sidewalk toward his office on Qarani Street.

In his mid-fifties, Parviz was balding, bearded, and bespectacled. While he wore a suit, similar to the other males traveling alongside of him to their offices, a necktie was not part of his apparel. The wearing of ties had been forbidden – or at least very severely frowned upon - by the late Ayatollah Khomeini. The practice was seen as a symbol of Western oppression - cultural and otherwise. And that was most certainly the case for government workers.

Across the boulevard to his right was one of Tehran's more infamous locations. It was called the *Nest of Spies* and the *US Den of Espionage*. It was, in other words, the former American Embassy. The walls of the facility, which encompassed a city block, were decorated with a variety of colorful anti-American murals - many of them highly creative. The garish depiction of the Statue of Liberty sporting a gaping death's head skull under its spiked crown was his favorite.

Nevertheless, the vast majority of Tehrani's paid the display little mind. After all, it had been there so long.

In its time, the former embassy had been the site of two mass assaults. The first of these occurred on February 14, 1979, when a group of Iranian Marxists invaded the grounds and took control. They held it for three hours before surrendering the property back to US authorities.

A sole Marine Security Guard was less lucky; he was taken from the embassy grounds, questioned and tortured for a week before being returned to American custody.

The second and more dramatic episode, composed of radicalized "students", took place nine months later on November 4, 1979. That action led to a hostage situation in which American diplomats were held captive for a total of 444 days. It ended on the day that Ronald Reagan was inaugurated as President of the United States.

Within the walls of facility was a revolutionary museum, intended to document the heinous acts of the old occupants.

Parviz turned the corner and walked another block and half north on Qarani Street until he reached his workplace. A few steps through a well-maintained garden area led him to the door of a sturdy masonry building. Few of the passers-by would have recognized it as a branch office of the MOIS. A guard in the lobby recognized him from the surveillance camera shot and buzzed him in through the hardened, ballistic-resistant doorway.

Reaching his office at last, Parviz doffed his jacket and settled in behind his desk. It was a fine piece of cypress furniture, as befitted his executive status. His work papers were already set out before him, awaiting his attention.

He was still in the settling in phase of the new job, as it had only been little more than a month since his return to Tehran. For the past three years, he had been assigned to the Iranian Embassy in Tbilisi, the capital of the former Soviet Republic of Georgia.

A male secretary, knowing his patterns, emerged from a side room with a cup of hot sweetened tea.

"*Sobh bekheir*," the man said. Good morning.

"*Salam*," Parviz said absently, nodding his appreciation.

The secretary lingered behind for several minutes, reviewing the schedule of the day's appointments. There was nothing unusual on the agenda.

After the secretary went back to his own work area, Shahriar Parviz appeared to study the first of many documents. But his mind was elsewhere. He was still mulling over his last meeting with the Frenchman who called himself Alban.

= SIX =

HAWK

Hollywood Cemetery
Richmond, Virginia
June 17, 2004

JD Tucker was standing on the sloping grounds of the historic Hollywood Cemetery. Despite its name, the graveyard had absolutely nothing to do with the motion picture industry.

The Org director was reverently admiring a thin, gray stone obelisk while enjoying the peaceful silence of the place. At the base of the aging monument was a simple inscription:

MAJ. GENL. J.E.B. STUART

Confederate States Cavalry
Wounded May 11th
Died May 12th, 1864
Aged 31 Years

JD Tucker was in Richmond to observe an ongoing surveillance detection/counter-surveillance training exercise. The course was being run over several days by a private group that was based out of the nearby King William County. A number of his Org people were going through it as a refresher training. They were intermixed within a fresh class of Diplomatic Security Special Agents from the US State Department.

Tucker absently heard a car door softly latch as it was pushed closed behind him. Leaving the vehicle, the expected new arrival crunched the gravel as he approached, coming to a stop a respectful distance alongside of him.

"Friend of yours, Boss?" the other asked as he paused to regard the obelisk.

"In theory. US Military Academy. West Point. Class of '54," Tucker muttered. "Eighteen fifty-four," he clarified with a tight smile. "A little before my time at the Academy."

Tucker reached down to wipe a smudge of accumulated grit off of the carved lettering. "Stuart died as a result of combat wounds that he received near the end of the war... The Battle of Yellow Tavern, just a few miles north of here," he said.

"So, I've heard."

"According to the story," Tucker continued, "he told people that he didn't want to survive the war if the South was to go down in defeat."

"I like the spirit of the man," the other offered.

"As do I," Tucker agreed, straightening up. "As do I." He paused to gaze down at the shallow rushing waters of the James River. "How are you doing these days, Hawk?"

"Doing good, Boss." He reached over to touch the obelisk himself. "Got your message last night. What's up?"

As was true with all of the JICSA case officers who were still in operational status, the man known as Hawk had never been to the Org's headquarters building in McLean. Chances were that he would never enter the building in the future on any official basis.

In keeping with their security SOP, Tucker opted to meet with him during the Richmond surveillance exercise, well away from prying eyes.

"I'm guessing you already heard about Chalice," Tucker said, still gazing at the Stuart monument.

"Yes sir, I have." He cast his eyes downward. "How's he doing?"

"Alive. Multiple surgeries pending. He'll be out of action for a good little while... Hopefully with no debilitating injuries. Although that last part is still unsure."

The Org director turned to regard his case officer as if seeing him for the first time.

Born in northeastern Oklahoma, Hawk was a full-blooded Cherokee in his late '40's. He stood at about 5'10', with a hulking build. His black hair was tightly pulled back and tied into a ponytail.

With his bronzed complexion and hooded brown eyes, he could pass - and indeed had passed - for a local in Latin America, Central Asia, and parts of East Asia itself. The solid biceps filling the sleeves of his polo shirt indicated some familiarity with the inner workings of a gymnasium.

Like the majority of Org case officers, Hawk had a background in military special operations. In his instance, it had comprised a full career, thirteen years of which were spent with the US Army's Intelligence Support Activity, or ISA. He finally retired out of the ISA with the rank of E-8, or Master Sergeant.

Created in 1981, after the failure of the Iran hostage rescue attempt (Operation Eagle Claw), the ISA had been active in such diverse geographic areas as Italy, Afghanistan, Africa, Honduras, El Salvador, Iraq, and Colombia.

In Tucker's view, the ISA had changed its cover names just about as often as his ex-wife had changed her mind. Over the years, they went by a variety of then-classified monikers such as Gray Fox, Cemetery Wind, Centra Spike, Yellow Fruit, Torn Victor, and many others. Beltway insiders often simply referred to them as The Secret Army of the North. The "North" as in Northern Virginia.

Tucker knew that the ISA had within their ranks a fairly small contingent of shooters/assaulters. As a former Delta commander, Tucker tended to look down his nose at that particular function. In his admittedly biased opinion, if you really needed some high-speed, low-drag, bad-ass door kickers, well, that's what Delta was for. And if Delta wasn't available, then you could always go down to the beach and find yourself a bunch of hyper-active Navy SEALs.

But the ISA's primary expertise was less in the field of direct action and more in what was called the intelligence preparation of the battlefield. This was performed via their cadres of electronic signals interceptors, the archaically named "knob turners", of the SIGINT Squadron, and the HUMINT agent handlers of their Operations Squadron. Hawk was a veteran of the latter ISA wing.

"You're still working that SORCERER case," Tucker said in a barely audible tone of voice. It was not a question.

"JADE SORCERER," Hawk amended. "Yes sir. I am."

"How's it going?"

Hawk shrugged noncommittally. "It's going. He's coming around."

"Push him harder," Tucker snapped coldly. "Quickly. I want to hit back at these Persian bastards. Real quick like. Not just for Chalice, but to send a message on behalf of US Intelligence as a matter of principle... Any pretext will do."

"Yes sir," Hawk answered, feeling the sudden change in emotion.

"I think that your folks back home would call this situation a *blood revenge*. Correct?"

"Yes, sir," Hawk replied, reflecting upon Cherokee lore. "That would be correct."

"Meyerhof will be in touch with details."

"Understood."

As Tucker started to leave, he paused and turned back to Hawk. "I'm sure you've heard the old expression: *Revenge is a dish best served cold*?"

"Yes Boss, I have."

The Org director shook his head with a grimaced expression. "I never believed in that shit," he growled. "Let's hit these bastards while the dish is still warm."

= SEVEN =

COMPAÑERO

El Salvador
1985

El Salvador is a small and densely populated country in Central America. Wedged in between Guatemala and Honduras, what it lacks in physical size it has more than made up for in its history of political violence.

In 1980, following years of festering tension, a civil war exploded onto the scene. What followed was a twelve-year horror mixing the worst features of rural warfare and urban terrorism.

Communist guerrilla atrocities were evenly matched by governmentally sanctioned massacres. All imaginable human rights violations prevailed, replete with rape, torture, death squads, and scattered body dumps. Those who sought to find innocents on either side of the conflict were equally doomed to dismay.

The Cold War opponents readily chose up sides. The United States sided with the Salvadoran government. Cuba and Nicaragua, and the rest of the Soviet Bloc, threw in with the FMLN - the Farabundo Marti National Liberation Front.

The FMLN took its name from a revolutionary martyr who was killed in 1932. It was actually an umbrella grouping of some five Leftist guerrilla families. One of these groups was the Central American Revolutionary Party or

PRTC. They dramatically emerged into America's public consciousness on June 19, 1985.

That evening, a handful of Marine Security Guards (MSGs) from the nearby American Embassy were gathered around a table on the sidewalk in front of a restaurant called Chili's. They were in a small, upscale shopping, eating and drinking area called the Zona Rosa.

Although the MSGs were in civilian clothes, they could not disguise their high and tight Marine Corps haircuts. Their identity was confirmed when a young boy approached them and asked if they were Marines from the Embassy. One of the MSGs proudly confirmed that, yes, they indeed were American Marines.

In tradecraft terms, this is called Target Identification. It is one of the final steps in the attack cycle, a time-tested progression that began with Target Selection and ended with Exploitation of the Act.

Very shortly thereafter, several vehicles screeched up to the curb. They disgorged a number of FMLN-PRTC gunmen, wearing a mixture of camouflage and civilian clothing. The shooters immediately opened fire with automatic weapons, spraying bullets into the bodies of the stunned and defenseless sidewalk customers. Their task quickly accomplished, the shooters leapt back into the awaiting vehicles and disappeared.

Left sprawled dead or dying on the sidewalk were four Marine NCOs. Their names were Dickson, Handwork, Kwiatkowski and Weber. The four young Marines hailed from Ohio, Wisconsin and Alabama.

Eight other people were killed as well, including American, Guatemalan, and Chilean civilians. A dozen more victims were left dazed and wounded - but thankfully alive.

The following month, the United States offered a reward of $100,000 for information leading to the arrest and conviction of the killers.

In a bit of black irony, when used as a point of reference, the attack site was casually referred to thereafter by the Embassy crowd as "*Chili's - Where the Marines were Killed*" almost as if it had become the formal name of the establishment.

* * *

Compañero is a common form of address among Leftist Latin revolutionaries, from the Cubans on down. One such Salvadoran revolutionary was known as Compañero Eladio. He was a relatively new member of the PRTC, having joined them earlier in the year.

As is common practice with such underground groups, new members such as Eladio were assigned to perform surveillance tasks. Street surveillants tended to be the least experienced and least trained members of the group. They also had limited exposure to the larger group. As such, they were deemed to be the most expendable.

Ostensibly a committed Socialist, Eladio explained his Mexican-accented Spanish by way of the fact that his parents had relocated to southern Mexico when he was still a young child. Dismayed by the lack of opportunities they found in the state of Chiapas, as well as the generally perceived discrimination against Salvadorans and other Central Americans, the family returned to their homeland after several years of effort.

Finding the situation in the land of his birth to be little better - and in many cases much worse than life in Mexico - Eladio gradually evolved from that of a peaceable Socialist to becoming an armed Revolutionary.

"Eladio," of course, was not his true name. Nor was it his true history. As was the case with all the others in his cell, it was his revolutionary war name.

"Hawk" was not his true name either. But it was the name by which he was known to his real-life compañeros in the US Army's shadowy Intelligence Support Activity.

As the war began, the United States established the MILGROUP, or US Military Advisory Group - El Salvador. Headquartered at the US Embassy since 1979, the goal of the MILGROUP was to train and modernize the Salvadoran military (ESAF). Less politely stated, the MILGROUP's objective was to jerk the ESAF out of their feudal comfort zone and somehow enable them to confront a rustic yet determined enemy.

Actively maneuvering on the other side was the Soviet Bloc. The Communist guerrilla fighters found help and sustenance from their allies in the Sandinista-controlled state of Nicaragua. Government raids uncovered weaponry in Salvador that had been supplied to the FMLN, via Nicaragua, from such diverse sources as Vietnam, Czechoslovakia, East Germany, Bulgaria, and Hungary.

Ever mindful of the painful Vietnam experience, the MILGROUP was limited to fifty-five advisors present in country at any one time. These were primarily comprised of Special Forces (Green Beret) troopers. In reality however, a rotating batch of additional TDY trainers and advisors routinely exceeded the authorized fifty-five-member ceiling on a regular basis.

Although an active-duty US Army soldier, Hawk was not one of these advisors. He was part of the undercover ISA effort that was designed to penetrate the ranks of the enemy. His objective was not to train the ESAF, but to directly undermine and destroy the FMLN leadership from within.

A fluent Spanish speaker since his early days in the Cherokee lands of Oklahoma, and ethnically blendable, Hawk was a natural choice for the job. Prior to being inserted in-country, he was supplied with a list of names of likely FMLN recruiters. It was not his first deep cover employment on behalf of the ISA, but it was the one in which he was to be the most isolated.

Purely by chance, one of the men that Hawk was able to contact outside of the capital, in the village of Antiguo Cuscatlán, was affiliated with the PRTC. The PRTC man, Jorge by name, was eager to attract fresh recruits as his organization was the smallest element of the FMLN family. A gregarious fellow, he tended to be not overly selective when he found candidates who were willing to risk their lives for the sake of the Revolution.

With minimal vetting, a period of indoctrination on Marxist theory, combined with tactical and weapons training, Hawk was recruited into the cell. After he was deemed to be successful in the basic tasks, Eladio was put to work on the streets of the capital - San Salvador.

It soon became apparent to Hawk that operational security was not a particular strength of the Leftists. Over the course of his PRTC service, he learned that the leader of the PRTC faction went by the *nom de guerre* of Commandante Hugo. It was common knowledge within the cell that the same individual was also identified as Mario Americo Duran. While not directly involved in the attack on the Marines, he was most certainly in the chain of command.

Hawk passed this data point along to his clandestine ISA contact at a papusaria eatery in downtown San Salvador. The contact, in turn, pushed the name up the chain to the ISA headquarters in Arlington, Virginia.

Before long, the Commandante Hugo moniker was linked to a true name: Americo Mauro Araujo-Ramirez. Further research indicated that Araujo-Ramirez, a sociologist in his mid-forties, was a senior Salvadoran Communist official.

Thanks to his verbose social contacts within the group, Hawk was able to elicit the war names of several of the other *compañeros* who actually took part in the Zona Rosa attack. As far as he could determine, the leader of the attack squad was a man called Ulises. Among the others were Macias, Ruperto, Pepe, and William.

An additional commando - called Julio - was himself killed during the attack. Whether Julio was the victim of PRTC crossfire or return fire from bystanders, no-one knew.

Another PRTC supporter - known as Alvarado - managed the safe house that Hawk himself had visited. Two others - Mauricio and Raul - used their property to conceal weapons for the fighters.

All of these names were duly pushed along to Arlington via Hawk's ISA contact.

A month after the Zona Rosa attacks, President Ronald Reagan authorized something called Operation Nine Iron. It was a highly classified retaliatory strike against remote FMLN camps. It consisted of gunship attacks and lethal raids from CONUS-based Army Rangers. The result was more than eighty FMLN killed with no American deaths.

On August 9th, while the FMLN was still reeling from the effects of Nine Iron, the door of Araujo-Ramirez' apartment was kicked in by Salvadoran police. The sociologist was roughly taken into custody. Within a month, four other men were arrested as part of the Zona Rosa investigation. Another seven conspirators evaded arrest.

* * *

After Araujo-Ramirez' arrest, what little that existed of the PRTC's internal security section swung into action. They correctly suspected a betrayal from inside the organization and were determined to eliminate the threat. They had three suspects: a certain Hector, a man called Reynaldo ... and another named Eladio. And Reynaldo had already disappeared.

Hawk quickly resolved that it was time for Eladio to do the same.

Three days later, Hawk drove a battered pick-up truck out of San Salvador and into the countryside. He left the truck on the side of the road next to an open field, unlocked with the keys in the ignition. He assumed that at least one *campesino* would be happy with the find before the night was out.

Within twenty minutes of his arrival, he heard the throbbing sounds of a helicopter's rotor blades. As he watched, an olive drab Huey rounded a distant volcanic slope and loomed into sight. It was coming in low just as the sun settled below the horizon. Hawk activated his strobe light and stood by for pick up.

No sooner had the skids of the UH-1B touched down on the soft grass than Hawk scrambled aboard and the ship lifted off again. Wordlessly, the pilot pivoted the nose about and set a northeasterly course for an airfield in Honduras.

Compañero Eladio was off the battlefield. Gone.

As for Araujo-Ramirez, he survived the war to become an elder political citizen of the nation. The FMLN itself was to emerge as in the years to come, as one of the major legitimate political parties in 1992.

= EIGHT =

PERSPECTIVE

McLean, Virginia
July 9, 2004

"So, bring me up to date on this Iranian thing," Angela said. "JD is starting to look at it as a top priority case."

She kicked off her shoes and unceremoniously dropped onto the sofa in her office. They were in the secure environs of the Org/GTA headquarters. "Lately my head's been so full of facts and figures about North Koreans, Iraqis and Latin Americans that I can't shake them loose."

Bart Landau flexed his shoulders to loosen up. "I think I can do that, Chief," he said. "What would you like to know?"

Angela yawned. "Just the down and dirty. What do I need to know to get my head around this JADE SORCERER case?"

Her subordinate analyst tugged his tie loose and nodded agreeably. "Well, I guess you could go as far back as the year 330 BC or so."

"I'm sorry... You said 330 BC?"

"Yeah. That's when Alexander the Great defeated the Persian army under Darius. The Battle of Gaugamela... It marked the decisive defeat of the Persians and the entry of the Greeks - or the Macedonians actually..."

"Let's bring it up to somewhere inside the twentieth century," Angela interrupted drowsily, her eyes closed.

Landau reddened slightly. "Okay. Well, no context then."

He leaned back in the chair next to her desk and started ticking off talking points on his fingertips.

"So. Number One. Iran is really not our friend. Not since the fall of the Shah in 1979. Good relations before that time, though. A lot of military sales and assistance to them in the good old days. Iran was our bulwark against the Soviets in the Gulf"

"Right," Angela mumbled almost to herself. "Goodbye Shah and good times. Hello Khomeini and bad times."

"Yes. And Number Two. They see their primary enemies as Israel and the United States. They hope to become at least a regional power and then expand from there. They think that having a nuclear arsenal would be a nice touch. Of course, we cut off nuclear cooperation with them in '79, but they are still pushing for it."

"Noted."

"Number Three. From a religious point of view, the Iranians like to see themselves as the leaders of the world Islamic movement..."

"And the Iranians are the..."

"Shi'ites," Landau supplied. "They're about fifteen percent of the world's Muslims. Aside from Iran, they're the majority in Lebanon, Bahrain and somewhere else. And Azerbaijan, I think... The other eighty-five percent of the world's Muslims are Sunnis."

"Right."

"Number Four," Landau continued. "With regard to our particular line of business, the Iranians replaced the Shah's SAVAK intelligence service with their competing organizations. The IRGC and the MOIS."

"Right," she repeated, resting a forearm over her eyes.

"Okay. And Number Five. The Iranians have been expanding their outreach with their support and training of the Party of God - Hezbollah - in Lebanon. Again, this is probably through MOIS' Department 15."

"Which gets us to San Juan, how?"

"It is odd," Landau agreed. "At the moment, their external interests seem to focus on Lebanon - specifically the Bekaa Valley."

"So, the leap to Puerto Rico is quite a stretch for them," Angela observed.

Landau paused. "Well, Iran has a Hezbollah presence quite a bit closer to home than the Bekaa Valley or Puerto Rico though," he said.

"Like where?"

"North Carolina."

= NINE =

JETHRO ENTERPRISES

High Point, North Carolina
July 14, 2004

The vehicle in question was a late-model minivan. Specifically, it was a Dodge Caravan, dark gray in color, bearing North Carolina plates. It carefully wound its way down a leafy two-lane road that terminated in an outlying, light industrial area.

At the end of the cul-de-sac was a collection of one and two-story buildings, all of which were fronted by a collective parking lot. The buildings were surprisingly bright and modernistic for what was usually called a warehouse district.

The van parked in front of the far end structure that was marked "Jethro Enterprises." After a few moments of pause, two occupants exited the vehicle and went inside. One of them had a heavy backpack slung over his left shoulder.

The attractive, dark-haired secretary/receptionist glanced up from her computer screen as the pinging door electronically announced the entry of the two men. She was wearing a pink polo shirt displaying the Jethro Enterprises logo.

"Leah," the older of the two men exclaimed happily. "There you are. And you are as beautiful as ever!"

"Mutt and Jeff," the secretary rejoined, with the hint of a Southern accent. "Two of my favorite guys."

Mutt, the driver of the minivan, pulled off his Florida Gators baseball cap and mopped the sweat from his brow. "Hot as hell outside for this early in the morning," he complained. "Freddy here?"

"Sure is," Leah said. "But are you here to see him or me?"

"You, of course, my love," Mutt smiled.

"Liar," she chuckled, punching a button on her phone. "Freddy," she called. "Customers up front."

The newcomers exchanged idle chit-chat with Leah until Freddy emerged from the back of the warehouse several minutes later. While the two visitors were ostensibly friendly and ever proper and polite, privately they always found it more than mildly amusing that a Jewess was involved in this business with them.

Freddy, a beefy middle-aged Hispanic, emerged from one of the back rooms. Sporting a shaved head and a bushy mustache, he was garbed in respectable biker chic attire: a black t-shirt, scuffed engineer boots, and faded blue jeans.

"Hey guys," he said, shaking each of their hands with enthusiasm. "What's happening?"

"Just the usual," Mutt said, wiping is face again. "Traffic is shit out there today."

"I hear you," Freddy sympathized.

"These long drives are getting harder to handle, the older I get," Mutt complained good-naturedly.

"You ain't shittin'," Freddy grinned. "That would make my ass tired too. But better you than me."

"Yeah... You got the stuff ready to go?"

"I do. You got the cash?" Freddy countered.

Mutt nodded, unslinging the backpack and dropping it onto Leah's desk.

Without further ado, Freddy unzipped the backpack and quickly confirmed that it contained the correct bundles of twenty and fifty-dollar bills. "Good to go," he confirmed. "Pull your van back in and we'll load 'er up for you."

There was a noisy ratcheting of gears as the wide garage door of the warehouse lifted open. Mutt waited inside as Jeff pulled the minivan around to the front and backed it in, finally killing the engine.

Once within the enclosure, the garage door came back down, ensuring privacy for all concerned.

Wordlessly, Mutt, Jeff, and Freddy quickly worked to load several large cardboard cases of cigarettes into the rear end of the Caravan. Ten minutes later, the deed was done.

"Okay buddy," Freddy said, shaking the hands of both Mutt and Jeff once again. "You're set. Long way to New York... Drive safely."

"Next time bro," Mutt replied, climbing into the passenger seat as Jeff fired up the engine once again.

The Caravan eased out of the warehouse bay as the garage door rolled back down behind them.

Leah waited until the visitors were well gone from the parking lot before she hit another button on her phone. "They're clear," she announced. The Southern accent was mysteriously absent.

Within moments, a concealed door in the rear of the warehouse bay opened and three men came out slinging their M-4 carbines over their shoulders. All were helmeted and wore ballistic vests with the gold lettering "POLICE - ATF" on the front and back. As in all previous meets, the tactical team was there to provide cover should the visitors decide to go violent for whatever reason.

Freddy now had a small Motorola radio in his hand. "Heads up everyone. Target loaded and moving," he declared. "You ready, One?... Ready, Two?"

"One on 'em and moving," came a reedy electronic voice.

"Two copies. Standing by," echoed another.

Leah was already tapping on her keyboard. She brought up a video program, then toggled "rewind" and hit "play." Within moments an audio-visual display of the meeting appeared on the screen, thanks to the variety of cameras and microphones secreted about the warehouse.

"Got it," she announced.

Freddy peered over her shoulder and nodded his satisfaction. "Okay. Now let's see what the boys on the road can develop," he muttered.

* * *

Several hours later, the team, minus the ATF tactical guys, was gathered about a table in the bay of the warehouse. Freddy, who in actuality was a Supervisory Special Agent from the Charlotte Field Office of the Alcohol, Tobacco and Firearms agency, led off the discussion.

"Well, first of all I'd like to welcome Leah's boss to our humble Day Tripper workshop here in High Point," he said, referring to the operation's case name. "SAC Kaczmar, good to have you here."

The man he was referring to was Jake Kaczmar, the Special Agent in Charge, or SAC, of the State Department's Diplomatic Security Washington Field Office. Tall with prematurely white hair and a trim mustache, he was professorial in appearance. This was despite the fact that he had served numerous tours as a Regional Security Officer in hardship and danger-pay posts overseas that were far from academic. The SAC job in Northern Virginia was to be his sunset tour, just prior to retirement.

"Happy to get out of the DC bubble and into the fresh air for a day or two," Kaczmar said, flashing a grin that had won him numerous allies over his career. "And also, to see what you are doing with our young lady here."

In contrast, Leah was a first-tour DS agent, one year out of Basic Agent training. Though lacking any prior law enforcement experience, it was clear to her supervisors that she had a keen analytical mind and was a natural for the job. Her primary role on this case was the protection of DS interests and the documentation of the illicit cash-for-product exchanges.

Truth be told, as a SAC, Kaczmar was torn about Leah's assignment. He knew that it was an important, worthwhile case. And it was good exposure in the larger law enforcement community for DS.

On the other hand, it pulled yet another scarce agent out of the "body pool" of available personnel in the capital region. He was feeling more than a little pressure from Headquarters to show some production for her time in what was then a fairly non-traditional role for DS agents.

While Leah was but one agent, between the demand for people to fill the slots in domestic protection, refresher training, overseas TDYs, weapons qualification, physical training, and leave, the drag on agent availability was significant. That was not to mention the fact that not everyone in Headquarters fully embraced the value of the domestic criminal program at all.

The case in question had been initiated by the ATF - formerly of Treasury, lately of the Justice Department. It was predicated on ATF's recognition that certain foreigners were engaged in a highly organized cigarette-smuggling enterprise. They were buying the product in North Carolina - a low-tax state - and selling them up north in high-tax states - replete with counterfeit tax stamps and at enormous profits.

The evidence indicated that the smugglers were, in the main, Lebanese nationals. It appeared that the profits, now in the millions of dollars of cash, were being channeled back to Hezbollah in Lebanon to fund their terroristic activities.

At the suggestion of an Assistant US Attorney, the man who would eventually prosecute the case in the Western District of North Carolina, ATF was encouraged to bring DS aboard. This was in recognition of the fact that the smugglers were using numerous false passports, illegally obtained travel visas and a slew of other fraudulent identity documents. The AUSA knew that DS could help amass even more felonies against the defendants when the take-down day came. And then there were the global resources of DS to be considered, via their extensive network of Regional Security Officers stationed in embassies and consulates abroad.

"So, what happened?" Freddy asked Jerrod, the surveillance team leader.

Jerrod, another Charlotte ATF agent, shook his head dismissively. "We picked him up coming out of here. As expected, he went out east on I-40 and then went off and up onto I-95 north. We went north with him a few miles further till he pulled off into a rest stop. But once he got there, he started displaying some very hinky behavior."

"As in?" Freddy prodded.

"He just sat there in the rest stop... Watching. No drinks. No getting out to stretch. No piss breaks. Just watching... For ten minutes."

"Okay."

"And there was another car there in the lot as well," he continued. "Dark blue Chevy sedan. Male and female in the front seat... They were there for ten minutes eyeballing the lot, even after our guy pulled out. Looked like a trained counter-surveillance team to me. Not amateurs. So, we broke it off right there."

"Got a photo of the Chevy?" Freddy asked.

"Rog."

Freddy nodded. "Agreed. Better to lose him there than to spook him altogether... We can put a car up further north on the next run in case Mutt tries this trick again."

"Same load this time?" Jerrod asked.

"Yep," Freddy said. "Always staying below the three hundred carton limit."

"What's the significance of that?" Kaczmar asked.

"Three hundred cartons. That's where it enters into federal criminal territory," Leah answered.

"I see," Kaczmar said. "Obviously, these are all cash transactions?"

"Tell him Leah," Freddy said, eager to keep his TDY DS agent in the game.

"Yes sir," she said. "Always cash. There is a Lebanese-run check-cashing store here in town. Looks like they are connected to this operation. The transport guys are using that to fill their backpacks with the cash that they bring here."

"Money-laundering too then," Kaczmar observed.

Freddy leaned forward on the table. "Money-laundering, tobacco smuggling, tax evasion, wire fraud, visa and passport fraud, terrorism, overseas connections running back and forth." He paused for a moment to let the weight of it all sink in. "Serious stuff. Serious prison time."

"Sounds like it," Kaczmar agreed.

"Sure would be nice if we could keep the active DS connection here. With Leah."

Kaczmar nodded. He could sell it to Headquarters. He *would* sell it to Headquarters. "You got it."

= TEN =

TECHNOLOGIE/PAN

Kirchberg District
Luxembourg City, Luxembourg
August 4, 2004

It was just after nine in the morning as Hawk, coffee mug in hand, settled in behind the desk. He was alone in the modest office of the firm called *Technologie Pan*, or "T/Pan." Stretching his arms and stifling a yawn, he carefully logged into the firm's desktop computer.

The T/Pan office was in the Kirchberg district of the capital. Located west of the Alzette River, it was in the central business area of Luxembourg City. Hawk had arrived in Luxembourg City the night before, after having departed Dulles and transiting through London. He was, admittedly, feeling a bit of the jet lag.

Behaving as the executive that he allegedly was, Hawk focused on the computer screen and began to examine the billing data and assorted correspondence that had accumulated since his last login from afar. The part-time receptionist had been given the day off to ensure the privacy of his endeavors.

As was fully expected, the demands on the business were limited. T/Pan was, after all, one of those rare corporations that did not aggressively seek new clientele.

Larger agencies than the Org had professional support officers who provided such necessary housekeeping functions. Given its relatively modest size, however, within the Org it fell to the case officers to do the administrative upkeep and maintain appearances. Hence, Hawk's presence in the Duchy.

The small, yet proud, Grand Duchy of Luxembourg traces its history back to the year 963 AD. Its national motto, "*Mir welle bleiwe wat mir sin*" translates as "We want to remain what we are." Notwithstanding that orientation, in the mid-1400s Luxembourg fell under foreign control, first of the Austrian Hapsburgs and then of the French. It was not until 1815 that it was able to finally declare its independence from France.

Independence aside, to this day France still maintains a significant level of political and economic influence in the affairs of the diminutive nation-state.

And that was one reason why a little-known company called Technologie/Pan, SA had been established as a legitimate business entity in Luxembourg nearly two years earlier. Although legally a Luxembourgish corporation, no secret was made of the fact that T/Pan was, for all intents and purposes, essentially a French-controlled firm.

Another reason for the location was the fact that Luxembourg - like Switzerland, the Caymans, Hong Kong, and other offshore locales - was highly attractive in terms of its banking secrecy laws. A founding member of the European Union, it also offered advantageous access to the other European markets. As such, it was a favored destination for several of the financial transactions of the Org's covert accounts.

By intent, there was no room in the corporate budget for advertising or serious outreach. Apart from a website, some social media, a recognizable office address, and the services of an occasional receptionist, the day-to-day business details of the firm were opaque by design.

In truth, T/Pan was neither a Luxembourgish nor a French commercial entity. It was a front, or a shell company, that had been specifically established by the Org to conduct a false flag operation against the Iranian target – ideally to include the placement of a controlled source in the hierarchy of the Iranian regime.

* * *

For many years previous, Iran had been suffering under a number of international economic sanctions. Unwilling to abide this situation, Tehran used its own intelligence organs to connect with foreign business interests in an attempt to subvert the sanctions.

Shahriar Parviz, he an officer of the MOIS, was part of this covert economic effort. As a senior official, his duties brought him into regular contact with the French business community, among others. Although the French were surely not alone in their interest to retain contact and profit from the Islamic Republic throughout the hard years of sanctions, they were found to be one of the more reliable partners.

However, European economic ties were not the sole concern of Parviz. Within his very limited circles of trust, he had already let it be known that he was personally and professionally festering under the presidency of Mohammed Khatami.

Although Khatami had been re-elected in 2001 as an ostensible liberal reformer, Parviz wondered what the president could actually accomplish, given the fact that the Supreme Leader, the Grand Ayatollah Ali Khamenei, oversaw everything.

Not the least of his issues was his unhappiness with the continuing political supremacy of what he viewed as the thugs of the Islamic Revolutionary Guard Corps over the professionals, like himself, of the Ministry of Intelligence and Security.

Parviz's concerns were not unwarranted. From the beginning of the Revolution, the IRGC had appeared as a highly favored and influential organization in Iran. This was often to the detriment of the MOIS.

While the IRGC was often described as a Praetorian guard, a knowledgeable analyst once aligned them more closely with the Comitatus tradition that once prevailed in the Eurasian steppes and within the pre-Germanic tribes in Europe.

In such olden-day structures, a sovereign lord was surrounded and secured by the members of his personal guard corps. The latter swore absolute loyalty and personal submission to the former. In return, the protectors were lavished with gifts and riches. Absent the ritualistic commission of suicide upon the death of their lord, the relationship was a fair description of the current-day IRGC.

The so-called Miles' Law established a fundamental reality of bureaucratic thought. The law declares that "*Where you stand depends on where you sit.*"

Shahriar Parviz clearly did not sit (or stand) with the IRGC. He saw no role, nor any interest for that matter, for himself in their numbers. In a previous tour, he spent nearly three years in Department 101, which coordinated intelligence matters between the MOIS and the IRGC. The assignment gave him a high degree of insight into the relationship. It only further soured him.

What he did see was an opportunity to take advantage of his access. Thanks to what is loosely termed as the "national resources" of the United States, his views on the matter were not a secret.

Studying what the Org knew about Parviz, they judged him to be an approachable target.

Everyone has vulnerabilities. In espionage shorthand, they are often described by the acronym of "MICE" - Money, Ideology, Compromise and Ego. More often than not, however, several of the factors overlap and reinforce each other.

With regard to Parviz's target package, it was clear that he was money-motivated; that much had been substantiated by the covert financial account that he established under a false identity in the Cayman Islands. Clearly, ego played a significant role as well. Disillusioned with the regime and his place in it, he was adjudged to be looking to finance a better life abroad in the days ahead.

And it was then that Hawk, posing as a deniable asset of the French Intelligence Service, reached out and made contact with the seemingly disaffected MOIS officer.

= ELEVEN =

THE CHAVCHAVADZE

Tbilisi, Georgia
February 25, 2003

A year earlier, Shahriar Parviz had been enjoying his tour in Tbilisi. Formally known as Tiflis, it was the capital of the nation of Georgia. And why not? It was an ancient, yet thoroughly modern city. Historical sites and well-provided restaurants abounded.

Despite the failing international support for the ailing Shevardnadze government, the social ambiance of the former breakaway Soviet republic was relaxed and comfortable.

Lodged in the heart of the Caucasus, Georgia bordered not only Russia, but Turkey, Armenia, and Azerbaijan as well. Roughly the size of West Virginia, Georgia considered Iran to be one of its major trading partners. This was not surprising, considering their histories were entwined for more than a thousand years, with Georgia having once been part of the Persian empire. As such, Tbilisi was a lucrative posting for an Iranian economics and trade development officer.

While Parviz presented himself to the host government as a commercial officer, his true role was that of MOIS station chief. One of the primary official responsibilities in his cover mission was the fostering of commercial exchanges - both overt and covert - with French business sources.

Although his growing disaffection for the Tehran regime had been simmering for the better part of a year, today was his tentative first face to face meeting with his ostensible contact with French intelligence. It was to be in the person of the individual calling himself Alban.

Despite his evident discomfort with his surroundings, a wry smile lit Parviz's face as he took them in. "A synagogue," he reflected in hushed tones of English, for he spoke no useful French and Alban had no Farsi. "A quite unexpected venue, I must say."

"Less chance of encountering one of your work colleagues, I thought," Hawk, who was operating under the pseudonym of Alban, replied.

"I believe you thought correctly," Parviz agreed. "My compliments."

They were idling in one of the outer rooms of the century-old Grand Synagogue of Tbilisi. It was not far from the Metekhi Bridge that spanned the river to the east. Nor was it a great distance from the site of the Iranian Embassy at Number 80, Chavchavadze Street.

As the senior MOIS officer under diplomatic cover, Parviz's office was at the Chavchavadze location. The Iranian ambassador, His Excellency Hossein Toosi, was fully aware of Parviz's true mission in the country. Toosi was, however, completely in the dark as to Parviz's secret affiliation with the Parisian envoy.

"It is a beautiful building," Parviz admitted, somewhat grudgingly.

"It is," Hawk nodded. "With a long history."

"But it belongs to the Jews."

"It does. No helping that, of course."

"And the French do not care so much for the Jews either," Parviz commented.

"Not really," Hawk said in agreement with his Iranian contact. "But, on another note, I found it interesting that your embassy is located on Chavchavadze Street," he offered. "Very ironic, in fact."

"Why is that?" Parviz replied. "Because the Chavchavadze were royalty? A noble Georgian family?"

"No," Hawk answered. "Because the latest member of the family line, David Chavchavadze, was a career spy with of the American Central Intelligence Agency. He was an officer in their Soviet targeting division for twenty years or so. And there you are. Right on the street of his name."

"Hmmm. I will report this back to my people. For what it's worth."

"Feel free," Hawk smiled. "Without citing the source of this intelligence of course."

"With all respect, Monsieur Alban," Parviz continued after a brief reflective pause. "I did not find your name on the diplomatic list of the French Embassy here in Tbilisi. Nor, if I can be indelicate, do you appear to be very French yourself."

Hak nodded agreeably. "As to your first concern," he replied. "I am not here with the embassy. I am based out of France. The Toulon area.

"And with respect to your second issue, I am a dual national - both French and Canadian. Born in Canada."

Parviz made a questioning face. "Canada?"

"I come from what the Canadians call *Les Premiers Peuples*, or the First Peoples," Hawk went on with the cover story. "My family are all of the Cree tribe. We are from Quebec. The Cree, as you may know, have had centuries-long connections with the French. My professional connections are even closer."

"I see."

"But if you are uncomfortable with this arrangement..." Hawk floated tentatively.

"No," Parviz objected quickly, having already received financial rewards through this connection. "A Canadian Indian man... Of course, no objection. Clever tradecraft. Very clever." His fingers fluttered dismissively. "Please continue."

"We have been at this particular business far earlier than the days of Cardinal Richelieu," he said. "We are confident with our practices."

"As have we."

Appearing to admire the artwork of the interior, Hawk continued. "So. We have already established sufficient contact with you through the Luxembourg company," he said.

"Yes."

"And that is the channel that we will continue to use, both for messages and for the transfer of funds to your account. Or accounts, as the case may be."

"Good."

"That firm," Hawk continued, "will from time to time openly offer bids on the defense contracts that your government has announced."

"I understand."

"But those bids will always come in a bit high," Hawk explained. "And they will never quite reach the expected performance requirements... In so doing, your office will be free to study them and then reject them in favor of more competitive bids."

Hawk passed a small computer thumb drive to the Iranian. "But the bid offers will also have coded phrases by which we will pass operational messages to you."

"Again, clever," Parviz agreed.

"We thought so."

Hawk glanced about to ensure their continued privacy in the synagogue.

"Other issues?"

"I am nearing the end of my tour here," Parviz confided, pocketing the thumb drive.

Hawk nodded. "As expected ... Where will they send you next?"

"Back home. A Tehran posting."

"Even better," Hawk replied with a genuine smile. "We may not be able to meet with you there, but hopefully you will be able to travel out from time to time."

"No doubt of that," the MOIS officer agreed.

"Have no fear, we will be in touch," Hawk said, touching the agent on his shoulder. He the added "As my people say, *Peyah-tik, nitotem.*"

Parviz looked at him questioningly.

"It's Cree," Hawk, provided. "It means 'be careful, my friend'."

Parviz nodded, with feeling. "And you as well. My friend."

= TWELVE =

BEIRUT AIR BRIDGE

Beirut, Lebanon
September 1997

For a good number of years, Beirut had the well-deserved reputation of being the terrorism and kidnapping capital of the world. This had especially been the case in the decade encompassing the years between 1982 and 1992.

From the American perspective, the most dangerous era began in the early '80s with the capture of a number of Western nationals. These included members of the American University in Beirut, several journalists, Christian clerics, and even embassy staffers. Apparently, no-one was safe, regardless of occupation or sympathy.

Most prominently among the victims had been Bill Buckley. He was the CIA Beirut Station Chief who was kidnapped in 1984 and brutally treated. He was either killed or died as a result of his injuries in 1985.

And then there was the case of US Marine Corps Lieutenant Colonel William Higgins. He had been serving as a member of UNIFIL, the UN peacekeeping force for Lebanon. Another abduction victim, he was taken from his vehicle at gunpoint in 1988 while traveling along a coastal highway.

Calling it an "open gift" to both Israel and the United States, 17 months later, Hezbollah released a video of a hanging body that was said to be that of Higgins. The Marine officer's remains were finally recovered south of the city in 1991.

Based on examination of the forensic evidence, both men had been relentlessly and extensively tortured prior to their deaths.

And now another DoD asset had gone missing. In this case it was a young Air Force NCO assigned to the embassy's Defense Attaché's Office. This time, it was Technical Sergeant Hank Bayard, a single, twenty-something Arabic linguist who was born in Clovis, New Mexico.

In October of 1996, in violation of standing policy, Bayard had slipped out of the embassy compound and accompanied an attractive Lebanese girl for drinks after work. Their destination was the bar area along the lively seaside promenade of the Corniche.

And that was the last that anyone in the US Government in officially knew of his whereabouts.

But after nearly a year, there was finally a lead in the case. It was, however, a sensitive lead that preferably should not be pursued by anyone identified with the embassy. The information was passed to the Army's ISA for follow-up and then assigned to Hawk who was, at the time, still a serving member of the ISA.

Fortunately, in terms of timing, the ISA learned that President Clinton's Secretary of State, Madeline Albright, was planning to make her first official visit to the capital of Lebanon. Flying into a war zone - something not unknown for a SecState - obviously necessitated an increased security presence. The ISA made arrangements to tag along with the security team.

* * *

The US Embassy in Beirut is situated on a long sloping hillside that overlooks the eastern Mediterranean. The main buildings, located for the most part at the crest of the hill, were shielded against hostile attack. The most visible evidence of the shielding were the slat armor anti-rocket screens protecting the various portions of the buildings.

One of the Assistant Regional Security Officers, or ARSOs, had just climbed the six flights of stairs that led to a platform atop a partially constructed tower that was part of the shielding. The tower, also known as the Crow's Nest, was situated about a quarter of the way down the slope from the main buildings. At the bottom of the hill sat a Lebanese Army tank, safeguarding the approach from that direction. In theory.

The midafternoon breeze coming in off the sea was fresh, and the vista of sparking blue-green waters below was nothing less than magnificent. It was hard to believe that all of this natural beauty could be set in such a violent locale.

Fairly new to post, the ARSO paused to soak in the impressive view. As he did so, a member of the Local Guard Force was busily pulling the protective canvas bag off of a .50 caliber heavy machine gun. Another LGF was prying open the lid of a metal ammo can. When they finished, the ARSO lifted the cover assembly on the .50, draped a belt of linked ammunition into it, and slammed the cover closed again. That done, he rested his hand on the charging handle of the gun. Ready to go.

Down below, the basketball court that doubled as a helicopter landing zone had just been freshly swept to remove any errant debris that might be caught up in the swirling rotor blades.

Within moments, a dull thud reverberated softly in the distance. The ARSO and the guards exchanged glances. A car bomb? A package bomb? An exploding gas line?

Who knew?

Too far away to care.

The ARSO's radio squawked, disrupting the quietude. It was a message from a colleague inside the chancery building. "Heads up out there," it said. "Package inbound."

"Copy that," the ARSO replied. Even as he set the radio back down on the rough cement ledge, he could see the dark gray speck looming in the distance out over the water.

The speck gradually enlarged as they watched. It was a US Army Blackhawk helicopter, a UH-60, that had earlier launched from the airport in Larnaca, Cyprus. It was skimming above the wave tops and boring through the humid air, heading steadily in their direction.

Known as the Beirut Air Bridge, the helicopter represented the American effort to bypass the notoriously insecure facilities at the Beirut International Airport by moving people back and forth directly from Larnaca to the protected grounds of the embassy.

The ARSO stood by on the .50 as the helicopter neared. His job was to provide suppressive fire, should any of the denizens in the neighborhood attempt to prevent the landing. So far, none had.

But today was another day - and it was still Beirut.

The noise level increased exponentially as the Blackhawk approached the coast. At last, the aircraft soared in above the water, flared out up and over the compound, and quickly settled down onto the concrete landing pad. As this would be a quick turnaround, the pilot idled his engines but did not shut them down.

Upon coming to a stop, the side doors of the aircraft rolled open and six men, all casually dressed in jeans and sweaty polo shirts, clambered out. Each was wearing an uninflated life vest and a rather odd-looking cloth helmet that was somewhat reminiscent of the Rocky the Flying Squirrel cartoons.

A number of embassy local employees emerged to assist the new arrivals with their baggage. Their baggage consisted of their personal belongings and several Pelican hard-side cases holding their weaponry, body armor, optics, and spare ammunition. The six passengers quickly doffed their life vests and cloth helmets, giving them to the crew chief ,who busily collected them by the armful.

The new arrivals were members of Diplomatic Security's Mobile Security Division, or MSD. They comprised a tactical support team that was dispatched in advance to reinforce the DS Secretary's Detail for Albright's impending visit.

In actuality, only five of the passengers were bona fide DS Special Agents. Hawk was the sixth member. He had recently joined up with them at the hotel in Larnaca. To the MSD team agents who were unaware of his specific mission, he was simply one of "Those Guys." Along for the ride and whatever else.

As the six men shuffled off of the pad, a handful of departing embassy staffers hurried past them, approaching the helicopter in a crouching scamper. The departees were then outfitted in the same protective flight vests and cloth helmets by the crew chief and strapped into their seats aboard the chopper.

Within minutes, the Blackhawk was once again aloft, turning and heading back toward Larnaca.

And all was silent once again.

= THIRTEEN =

NASTY BOYS

Beirut, Lebanon
September 1997

Given the differences between the overriding schedules of the SecState and that of the Beirut Air Bridge choppers, the MSD team was left to cool their collective heels in the TDY quarters of the embassy - the so-called "Tango Inn" - for nearly a week prior to her arrival.

After several nights at post, the senior Regional Security Officer, or RSO, offered to escort them out for dinner at a local restaurant. The bored and distracted MSD agents, who featured themselves as highly trained action guys, were more than happy to oblige.

However, dining out in Beirut in 1997 was not a simple process. No embassy staff were permitted to leave the compound on their own - the case of Hank Bayard notwithstanding.

Embassy staff diners were permitted to go out, but could only do so in groups. And those groups had to be accompanied by a detachment of the embassy's local bodyguards.

The bodyguards, under the command of the RSO, were nick-named the "Nasty Boys." Reveling in their Americanized name, the Boys even produced and sold t-shirts, replete with their logo, which were popular with staff and visiting TDY'rs alike.

On the evening of the dinner, the MSD team, including Hawk, crammed themselves into an armored Chevy Suburban for the short trip north of the embassy to the selected restaurant.

Ahead of their vehicle was a lead truck crewed by the Nasty Boys. The RSO was up there riding in the right front seat. More notably, behind them was another Nasty Suburban. That one, however, had a ring-mounted light machine gun on the roof of the vehicle with one of the helmeted bodyguards manning it.

"Hell of a production just to go out to eat," one of the agents remarked, craning his neck to stare at the gun truck behind them.

"All the better to make sure that you are to come back from eating", the team leader replied flatly.

"All buttoned up back there?" came the RSO's voice over the radio.

"Yeah, Chief," replied the Nasty's Lebanese shift leader in the gun truck behind the Suburban.

"'Kay. Let's roll."

The small motorcade pulled out of the compound and headed north. They quickly left the coastal area and began moving inland toward the nearby suburbs. The trip, despite the inherent drama, was uneventful. Upon reaching the restaurant some fifteen minutes later, the MSD team was surprised to see how modernly upscale and apparently peaceful the place was.

While the MSD agents were settling in around a communal table and ordering drinks, Hawk made his excuses and went to the bathroom.

The ISA operative had a .45 caliber Glock pistol tucked into the back of his waistband. Two spare magazines were in either pocket of his light jacket. A folded Spyderco knife was clipped to the inside of his waistband. He was also carrying a cellphone that had been provided by the embassy's Defense Attaché, an Army lieutenant colonel, who was aware of the task at hand.

Leaving the bathroom, Hawk exited through a rear door. Once outside of the restaurant, he carefully ambled away for a couple of blocks and then hailed a taxi.

"Corniche," he told the driver. "Bar Blu."

* * *

As he traveled toward the Corniche and the latest instance of a possible terroristic kidnapping event, Hawk's recollections focused on another, more extreme historical example of counterterrorism that originated in the same general neighborhood.

A little more than a decade earlier, in 1985, members of Hezbollah had snatched four Russian diplomats from outside of their embassy in Beirut. In return for their release, Hezbollah demanded that Moscow pressure one of the pro-Syrian militias to cease their shelling of Hezbollah supporters further north along the coast.

When Moscow failed to respond to their demands, one of the captured diplomats, Arkady Katkov by name, was found shot to death in a nearby field.

This time the Russians did respond.

The Russian response however came via the good offices of the KGB. Moving swiftly, an undercover KGB team returned the favor by kidnapping a relative of one of the Hezbollah leaders. The unfortunate relative was then spirited away to a secluded place where he was castrated before being dispassionately killed with a bullet to the head.

Afterward, the man's severed body parts were sent to the Hezbollah leadership with a warning that more was yet to come. And it would involve still other members of their own families. Unless...

Message received and understood. The three remaining Russian diplomats were released, alive, in the vicinity of the

Russian embassy. No further Russian nationals were kidnapped in Beirut.

While Hawk vastly differed with the philosophy of the old KGB, as well as their SVR successors, he honestly could not find fault with some of their tactics.

* * *

At his request, the taxi driver dropped Hawk off a block or so away from Bar Blu. He wanted the opportunity to assess the vibes of the surroundings as he approached the last known location of Tech Sergeant Hank Bayard.

From the personnel assessment file that he had reviewed, Hawk knew that Bayard was a fairly unremarkable Air Force noncommissioned officer. He was unmarried, smart, and politically aware. He was generally thought to be lacking in religious upbringing. Colleagues saw him as somewhat idealistic.

Interestingly, several of his fellow airmen stated that Bayard took to his Arabic studies at the Defense Language Institute, or DLI, in California with alacrity. If anything, some said, he seemed to be a bit sympathetic to the revolutionary causes to which they were exposed in their area studies program.

Hawk was well familiar with DLI. Thanks to the Army, or more specifically the ISA, he had attended a thirty-six-week French language program at the very same location in Monterrey. In his case however, while he graduated with a proficient ability in the language, he had not developed any similar sympathies for foreign cultures that apparently attracted the missing Bayard.

As he entered the establishment called Bar Blu, it was clear that any devout Muslim pretensions were left behind on the sidewalk. In keeping with the amorphous character of Lebanon, this was a trendy drinking and socializing establishment that would not be unknown in any West European locale.

Taking a seat at the bar, he ordered a glass of the local red wine, a Ksara cabernet. Hawk nursed the first glass, absorbing the nuances of his surroundings. When the barman brought him a refill, Hawk asked as to the whereabouts of a woman named Vardah.

There is some debate as to whether the world's oldest profession could have been claimed by Hawk and his associates, or by Vardah and her associates. Nevertheless, she was the woman with whom Bayard had a personal arrangement. And she was the one that Bayard had left the embassy to meet on the last day of his known schedule.

The barman looked at his watch. "Not here yet," he replied. "But, I think, she will be."

Hawk folded several Lebanese pound notes and slipped them across the bar. "I would like to know when she arrives."

The barman nodded and deftly pocketed the cash.

As Hawk bided his time at the bar, he turned his attention to the TV set on the wall. It was tuned to a satellite station called Al-Jazeera. Broadcasting out of Doha, the capital of Qatar, the station was scarcely a year old. Even so, it was already gathering a reputation in Western circles of providing favorable coverage to the "other side" in the war against terror. Given the political turmoil, he wasn't surprised to see it in downtown Beirut.

Hawk was still sipping his second glass of wine forty minutes later when the barman caught his attention. Wordlessly, he gestured to his left with his chin.

Stunning was the word that first came to Hawk's mind. Standing at slightly over five feet tall, the woman had a trim figure that was accentuated by a black leather mini-skirt and a green satin blouse. Her sharp, aquiline features were softened with a mane of long, chestnut colored hair. She returned his gaze with feline shaped eyes.

"I am Vardah," she announced in English. "You were asking for me?"

"I was," Hawk replied. He motioned to the open stool that he had been jealously guarding next to him. "My name is Eladio. Please sit... May I buy you a drink?"

Without ordering, the barman appeared with a white wine spritzer. Hawk noted that it appeared to be heavy on the soda water and light on the wine.

"*Vardah,*" he said. "That is Arabic for Rose. Yes?"

"I am told so. Yes."

"You are very pretty."

"And you are a handsome American," she observed, taking a first sip of her drink.

"Mexican," Hawk told her. "But I live in America. Not so unusual."

"That is what I hear," she said. "Congratulations."

She took another sip. "And why are you now in Lebanon?"

"Working," he replied.

"Me too."

Hawk toyed with his wine glass as Al-Jazeera switched to a story of Palestinian unrest in the territories. The screen revealed footage of stone -throwing protesters waving their arms angrily and retreating under exploding clouds of tear gas.

"I was wondering," he offered, purposely making small talk. "How is life here now? In Lebanon? For the people?" Vardah shrugged. "Better than during the war. But always troubles... If not the Christians, then the Muslims. If not the Sunni, then the Shi'a. If not the Israelis, then the Syrians... Never peaceful."

She turned to look directly at him. "That is our normal."

"And you," Hawk asked. "Where are you in all of this?"

She took another drink of her spritzer. "As you Mexicans say, I am an *independentista.*"

"That's the Puerto Ricans," Hawk corrected.

"Same thing."

Hawk paused to digest that for a moment. "It's kind of loud here. Is there somewhere else that we can go? Privately?"

Vardah smiled and drifted her fingertips lightly across the top of Hawk's thigh. "Of course," she smiled.

Hawk left a generous tip on the bar and slipped off of his stool to follow her lead.

* * *

They didn't go very far. Vardah took Hawk across the street from the Bar Blu to a hotel and then up to the third floor, where she had a key to one of the rooms.

Upon entering the room, Hawk found it to be small and tidy, not unlike that expected of a European youth hostel. Without being too obvious, he peered about the room and bathroom to ensure that they were truly alone. He then ensured that the door was firmly closed and locked.

"Satisfied?" Vardah asked, watching his activities.

Hawk turned his attention to her with a slight smile. "Very much so."

"And, so now we are in a private place," she said. "As you asked."

Without further pretense, Vardah unbuttoned her blouse and allowed it to fall open, revealing a flimsy lace bra. She was beginning to shrug out of her skirt when Hawk stopped her.

"No," he said. "Not just yet. I'd like to talk to you first."

"Talk?" she repeated with a coy half-smile. "You have to pay for that as well."

"Of course. How much?"

Vardah quoted him a price that was obviously inflated for the rare Western customers. Hawk nodded agreeably and passed her another collection of pound notes.

"So. Talk," she said, sitting on the bed and secreting the money in her purse.

Hawk pulled up the single wooden chair and sat in front of her. "I am looking for information about an American. Someone that you may have known."

Vardah remained unexpressive.

"His name is Bayard. Hank Bayard. Or Henry Bayard. He worked at the American Embassy here."

She shook her head. "I do not know him."

The denial was unsurprising.

Hawk withdrew a couple of photographs from an internal pocket of his jacket. He put the first one gently on her lap. It was of a young American in a dark blue US Air Force dress uniform. "That's Bayard," he said. "A few years ago."

Vardah glanced at the photo absently. "No," she said. "Sorry."

Sighing, Hawk placed a second photo on her lap. It was of an obviously happy man and a beautiful, bikini-clad woman. They were mugging for the camera on a sunny, sandy beach.

"That was taken last year. Specifically, in August of 1996. Mackenzie Beach. Cyprus," Hawk intoned. "That is a picture of you and Bayard on a quick weekend vacation just outside of Larnaca. No?"

When she remained silent, he added, "We know that he was last seen at Bar Blu one evening last October. With you. No doubt of that."

Vardah studied the picture momentarily before handing it back to Hawk. "You said you are here working... Who are you working for?"

"For Bayard's family in New Mexico."

"For his family?"

"Yes," Hawk answered. "I'm a private investigator. Their son has been missing for a year."

"And?"

"They feel that since the US Government isn't doing anything to find him, they will try to do it themselves."

"Just you are doing this?"

"And my partners."

"All the way from there to Lebanon," Vardah mused with a half-smile. "His family must have money."

"Enough," Hawk confirmed.

When she drifted back into silence, he decided to try another tack. "Did you have any feelings for him? For Hank? Any feelings at all?"

"I had feelings for him," she quickly snapped. "Yes, I liked Hank Bayard. He was good to me. He treated me well."

"Is he dead?"

"Dead?" Vardah repeated. She looked away. "Maybe dead to the old ways... Your ways... Maybe he found a new way of life. A better way."

"A better way," Hawk repeated. "Perhaps in the Bekaa Valley?"

Vardah looked up quickly. The Bekaa Valley was a notorious outlaw stronghold to the east and northeast of Beirut. It was an area not unknown to Hezbollah.

"The family has heard reports that Bayard was seen in the Bekaa," he pressed. "Just a few months ago."

She remained painfully silent.

"Vardah," Hawk said softly. "The family deserves to know whether their son is dead or alive... Their only son... The man who treated you so well."

She glanced up briefly and turned her gaze down once again.

"If one of your family members vanished in a foreign country," he delved once again. "Wouldn't you want to know? To have some sort of closure? Even if it were bad news?"

Shaking her head, Vardah reached for a pad of paper on the end table. She scratched out a few notes and handed it to Hawk. "This is what I know... Maybe a village in the Bekaa called Nahle... Maybe a man there called Yaqub. That is all."

Hawk tucked the note into his pocket, sensing that he had gotten all that was possible from this source at the moment. He thanked her, passing along a bit more cash for her assistance.

Vardah partially reclined on the bed as Hawk made to leave, allowing the folds of her open top to gently part once again.

"Hey, Mexican," she breathed, slightly above a whisper. "There is no reason for you to leave this soon."

"You don't know how much I wish that could be so," Hawk said, resting his fingers briefly against her cheek.

* * *

Hawk peered about cautiously as he stepped back out onto the sidewalk. Night had fully fallen by then and, as is the case everywhere, it provided cover for those who would do people ill. Especially in Beirut.

Moving casually, he put a bit of distance between himself and the hotel. Pausing in the shadows of an alleyway, he pulled out the embassy cellphone and made a call to the Defense Attaché. "Ready for pick-up in ten minutes. Location as discussed," he said.

"We'll be there," the voice on the other end replied.

Hawk gave a final glance back at the hotel as he continued along on foot. It occurred to him that the Tango Inn would be feeling especially lonely that night.

= FOURTEEN =

MEDVED

Cheraw, South Carolina
August 20, 2004

The man in question was a newcomer to Cheraw. Perched along the narrow Pee Dee River in Chesterfield County, the rural community of Cheraw billed itself as "The Prettiest Town in Dixie." And maybe it was.

The newcomer parked his rental car in front of the quaint little breakfast place called Mary's Restaurant in the small downtown area.

Exiting the vehicle, he did not call much attention to himself. Nor did he wish to do so. Thickly built and in his late fifties, he had a full head of graying blond hair that flowed generously over his ears. He sported a beard to match.

He fit in.

But perhaps his most pronounced feature was a pair of flinty, ice-blue eyes and a cold stare that he could not hide.

A former Army Green Beret sergeant, he was a veteran of the Vietnam Conflict. There, he served as a commando in the shadowy, cross-border reconnaissance group called the Military Assistance Command/Vietnam - Studies and Operations Group, or MACV-SOG.

SOG had a storied history of daring heroics in the war. And, unfortunately, they suffered a very high rate of casualties for their efforts. Many of their numbers, both

Americans and Indigenous personnel, were lost over the fence – as it was called. The casualties were a result of clandestine missions into the denied areas of Laos, Cambodia and even into North Vietnam and China itself.

Those who survived the vicious, close-contact version of war carried the lessons - and the bloody memories - of the war with them forever more.

The newcomer settled into one of the tables at Mary's. He had a number of identities, some of which even he had forgotten. Known to his friends and colleagues simply as Bear, his true Christian name was Paul Michael Medved.

Following his discharge from the Army, Bear had returned home to his native Pittsburgh. There he eventually married, fathered a child, and became a sworn officer with the Allegheny County Police Department. Within the ACPD, he quickly progressed from the role of rookie uniformed patrolman into what was to become a long-term stint as an undercover narcotics detective.

As a newly-minted narc, he found himself mixing easily with the criminal street element. His personality, already coarsened and textured by his SOG experiences, adapted and evolved accordingly.

After several years as a seasoned undercover County narc, Bear was working overtime on still another case late one rainy evening. It was on the Southside district of Pittsburgh. The target was yet another run-of-the-mill doper. In this instance, the target was a grad school chemistry student who was producing his own brand of the MDMA drug called Ecstasy.

Upon completion of his meeting with the chemist, Bear learned his wife and child had just been killed in a senseless traffic accident. They were victims of a simple drunk driver. No more, no less.

Bear - finding himself once again alone in the world - doubled down on his efforts to take the fight to the enemy on the streets. In so doing, he moved ever further away from his moorings as a conventional law enforcement officer. In the course of the voyage, he drifted closer to the more relaxed morality mindset of the mercenary.

It was then, while on operational loan from the Allegheny County Police to the Drug Enforcement Administration, that he came to the attention of JICSA - the Org. Fully appreciating his unconventional skills, the Org appealed to his true nature and offered him an alternative career option. He accepted.

Since then, Bear had been an occasional agent, or asset, of the Org, working on an as-needed basis. Throughout his various operations, his single Org case officer had always been the man that he knew only as Chalice.

Bear's affiliation with the Org had involved him in covert operations as far afield as Colombia, Haiti, and China. The last mission reached into the secluded confines of North Korea.

Since his last contract in northeastern China, Bear had devoted his full-time efforts to the private security and consulting agency that he ran out of a small office in the suburbs south of Pittsburgh.

Lately remarried, he had promised his new wife that his days of seeking adventures overseas were well over and done with. That was until the call came three days earlier, asking for a meeting.

Expecting to see the familiar face of Chalice, Bear suddenly alerted to the here and now as he caught sight of the figure stepping through the doorway of Mary's.

Judging from his muscular stature, as well as his sharply etched dark features and black ponytail, the man could well have been a Cartel envoy. Possibly someone who came to this nondescript Southern town to deliver a final message of retribution from the old narc days.

As he watched, the man slowly weaved his way between the tables and continued in his direction. In response, Bear slightly dipped his right shoulder, allowing his hand to drift below the tabletop. There was a 9mm Glock 26 pistol in an elastic holster that was strapped to the inside of his left ankle.

The Glock already had a round in the chamber. If he had indeed been set up for a hit, there might be time to get the "Baby Glock" into action. But maybe not.

In any case, it certainly would light up an otherwise sleepy morning in a quiet rural town.

Wordlessly, the unsmiling new arrival sat down across from Bear and calmly folded both hands together on the tabletop.

"Nice little village they have here," he said, without any formalities. "Don't 'ya think?"

"Yes," Bear answered warily. The Glock was now in his hand under the table. His finger was resting gently on the trigger. "Yes, it is."

"You've been to that St. David's Episcopal Church down the way?" the other continued in a conversational tone of voice.

"Yeah," Bear said, relaxing with the sounds of the agreed recognition protocol. He slipped the gun under his thigh against the wooden chair. "Old place. They have a veteran of the French and Indian War buried in the churchyard there."

The other man nodded and reached out to shake Bear's hand. "Hawk," he said.

"Bear... But I assume you already know that."

Hawk grunted affirmatively.

An elderly waitress appeared from nowhere to fill their cups with steaming black coffee. She affectionately called them each honey, exuding old-fashioned Southern courtesy, as she took their breakfast orders.

Bear waited as the old lady retreated back across the cracked linoleum to the kitchen area. "Guilty," he said at last.

"Of what?"

"Profiling," Bear smiled tightly. "For a moment there, I thought you might be a shooter. From Down South."

"No offense taken. Sometimes profiling can save your life," Hawk observed. "But I'm glad that you gave me the benefit of the doubt."

"You'd do the same for me," Bear offered. "I guess."

Getting no response, Bear peeled open a container of creamer and dumped it into his coffee. "Cheraw. Chesterfield County. South Carolina," he mused. "Could you have found a more out of the way place for a meeting?"

"Thanks," Hawk replied, taking it as a compliment. "How'd you get here?"

"Took a flight out of Pittsburgh to Charlotte yesterday. Rented a car. Spent the night up there. And here I am... You?"

"I have business in the region."

"Okay... So, generally speaking, why are we here? What's the deal?"

Hawk paused as another customer eased passed them on the way to the men's room. "We have another contract opportunity coming up," he continued in a subdued tone of voice. "Could be several months in length. Maybe a little more."

"Yeah?" Bear replied. "And where's Chalice?"

"Side-lined for now."

"Why?" Bear pushed.

"Medical reasons."

"Medical reasons... What happened to him?"

Hawk held his gaze flatly. "You don't have any reason to know that right now."

Bear stirred his coffee aimlessly, slightly miffed at the rebuke, but understanding the rationale. "So then, I guess you're taking it upon yourself to get the band back together again?"

"More or less. With authorization... You gonna be available?"

Both men held their counsel as the waitress came back with two plates of fried eggs, ham, and grits. Buttered toast on the side.

"Looks just great, ma'am," Hawk said, glancing up and smiling for the first time since his entry. "Thank you."

"You fellas enjoy it now," she replied, moving on to a table of new arrivals closer to the door.

Bear broke off a piece of toast and dipped it into the soft yellow egg yolk. "Just got married a few months ago," he said.

"I know."

"Told her, Kelly's the name, that I wouldn't be taking any more security contracts that involved overseas work. Like in, *any* overseas work."

Hawk piled a slice of his eggs and ham onto the toast and took a bite of it. "Understood," he said. "So, what did you tell her about this?"

"That there might be a job involving travel to Miami. Texas. The Southwest. Like that."

Hawk nodded, reaching for his coffee cup. "Well, that much might be true. At least."

Bear regarded Hawk warily as he continued to eat. "You know a lot about me," he said, finally breaking the silence. "And since we're bonding and all, why don't you tell me a little something about yourself."

Hawk took another sip of coffee and noisily clattered the cup back onto the saucer. "I'm not a Colombian, if that's what's worrying you. I'm all American. Even more than you. Full-blooded Cherokee Indian. Born in Oklahoma. Retired NCO, US Army. Now working with our mutual friends. Like you."

"A lot in common then," Bear reflected.

"I thought so."

"Cherokees," Bear repeated thoughtfully. "Aren't your people mainly from North Carolina? The Appalachians. Forcible removal to the west. Trail of Tears and all that."

Hawk raised an eyebrow. "You are well-read."

"For a White boy."

"You know," Hawk continued, "for the Cherokee people, geographic directions were culturally linked with both colors and fates. Destinies."

"As in?"

"The color associated with the north was blue. That equaled trouble."

"Yes?"

"The south was white - peace. And the east was red - victory."

"And west?"

"The west, the direction of the Trail of Tears, was bad. It was associated with the color black. And with death."

"Sorry to hear that," Bear said.

"Not only that. Some Cherokee feared that certain wild animals were capable of casting evil spells upon them... Can you imagine what the worst of the animals was?"

"No idea."

"Bears," Hawk supplied.

"Huh. Well, my apologies to you and your ancestors," Bear smirked, returning to his breakfast.

"All of my sad history aside, what do you think of the offer?"

Bear paused. "Sounds possible... Not that Kelly would agree."

Hawk dug further into his plate of food. "Give it a little thought," he said. "If you're interested, meet me in the graveyard at that St. David's Church around fourteen hundred this afternoon. I'll fill you in on the details."

Bear bobbed his head and continued eating. But he already knew.

How could he resist?

= FIFTEEN =

KITUWAH

The Kituwah Mound
Cherokee, North Carolina
August 22, 2004

Having firmed up arrangements in Cheraw with his newly reacquired asset, Hawk felt comfortable in taking an unauthorized side trip on his way back up to the Washington area. That journey took him into the Smoky Mountains in the western regions of North Carolina.

A good half day out of Cheraw, he reached his destination. It was a few miles outside of the small town of Cherokee, near the Tuskegee River.

After pulling to the side of the road, Hawk climbed out of his rental SUV and pulled a chilled can of beer from a small cooler as he did so. Cracking the top, he leaned back against the vehicle and took a sip as he absorbed the view.

He had been there once before, having traveled to the site with his parents around the age of eight or nine. The memory of that trip was fading and, in his view, in need of refreshment.

Hawk recalled his elders telling him tales of the origin of the world, in the view of the Cherokee ancestors. To them, the world was originally a floating island in a great sea of water. The earth, they said, was then attached to the sky by four stout cords.

Based on his own experience, Hawk strongly doubted that last part. But he did agree with the historical fact that the population of his forbears was centered right here in the mountains of North Carolina. This included stories of their battles with the so-called Moon Eyed People. If true, they were a frightening race of pale-skinned archaic humanoids with large eyes who lived below ground and fought the Cherokee warriors by night, only to be defeated in the end.

From the side of the road, Hawk was looking at an actual ancient American historical site. Yet for all of its significance, there was not much to see. It was a small, protected mound of earth some 170 feet in diameter and a scant five feet high.

Although Hawk was born in Oklahoma, the genesis of his heritage could be found here. It was called the Kituwah Mound.

The Eastern Band of the Cherokee Tribal Council purchased the land in 1996 to preserve it from further development, its dimensions having already been significantly trimmed by past activities. It sat on a 309-acre site that was on the National Register of Historic Places.

Archeologists had traced the provenance of the hallowed mound back some 10,000 years. Within its environs, they had discovered 15 confirmed burial plots to date. Another thousand or more graves were believed to be yet uncovered in the immediate area.

The ground before him was said to be the very heart of the Cherokee culture. It was where the Creator had supposedly given fire to the Cherokee people. The sacred, eternal fire had supposedly burned atop of a larger version of the mound, having been carefully tended to in a special council house.

This would have been the locus of the old ways. The merger of ancient power coupled with the loss of actual power. The reality of submission. The all-night vigils of the bodies of the recently dead to protect them from witches, as well as the fear of weakness emanating from the Christian religion.

Hawk shook his head. He had heard tales of the ground before him as being equivalent of The Vatican for the Cherokee people. Sadly, there was not much to show for it now.

A white historical roadside marker told the story as tersely as possible. It read:

KITUWAH
Cherokee mother town.
Council house stood on mound here.
Town was destroyed in 1776 by
Rutherford expedition.

The 1776 reference was correct, though not overly informative. It reflected the strategically unfortunate decision of the Cherokee people to cast their lot with the side of the British and their Loyalist militias at the time of the Revolutionary War.

Not surprisingly, the rebellious American forces took a dim view of this. They sent troops, directed by the Irish-born General Griffith Rutherford, to show their displeasure in the most direct means possible. The result of the expedition was the destruction of several Cherokee towns in the area.

Worse was yet to come.

Around 1820, a group of Cherokees, estimated to have been less than a thousand, found their way into the region of what is now East Texas. While it was then a territory of Mexico, it was being heavily colonized by American settlers.

Although the Cherokee fancied themselves as "the Principal People", the white Texans regarded them as less so. Nevertheless, the white Texans, or Anglos, regarded the Cherokee as a civilized Indian tribe; far more so than some with whom they were engaged in a constant state of low level warfare. The relationship was such that, in 1836, the President of the newly independent country of Texas, Sam Houston, signed a treaty of peace between the two parties.

It was not to last, however. In 1839 another Texas President named Mirabeau Lamar declared that the treaty was worthless and, as such, he ordered the Cherokee out of Texas altogether. They refused.

A battle later ensued at the Neches River with the outnumbered Cherokee nearly being massacred. Survivors of the engagement made their way out of Texas and into the safer environs of Mexico and Oklahoma.

Meanwhile, back East, the so-called Trail of Tears, to which Bear had earlier referred, began in 1838. It was based on President Andrew Jackson's promotion of the Indian Removal Act of 1830. The Act was designed to move native populations out of the populous southeast and into the empty west. By way of a historical footnote, the Act was opposed by a famous Tennessee congressman named Davey Crockett.

As a result of the Removal Act, between 16,000 and 17,000 Cherokees were evicted from their homelands and forced to move. The trip lasted more than a hundred days. An estimated 4,000 of their number died along the route, victims of disease, hunger, and exposure.

Reflecting back on his meeting with JD Tucker at the Richmond cemetery, the general's reference to blood revenge was not far off. It referred to the belief that a death (or an attempted death in this case) required a reply in order to restore the natural balance between the physical and the spiritual worlds. That was to be his responsibility.

Despite their history, Hawk was far from the first Cherokee to seek a career in the Army. As far back as World War I, a group called the League of the Iroquois, seeing itself as a sovereign nation, declared war on Germany and entered the US Army as "allies." Thanks to their action, in

1924 Congress passed the Indian Citizenship Act which recognized Indians as US citizens.

Ironically, as Hawk knew, a prominent figure involved in this episode was also the last Confederate general to surrender at the end of the Civil War. He was himself a Cherokee. The man's name was Stand Watie. Born in Georgia, Watie was a planter, who then owned dozens of slaves. He was not alone in the practice, as the Cherokee at the time held something close to 5,000 Africans as slaves.

In 1835, Watie did something that made him unpopular with many of his fellow Cherokees. He and three of his relatives agreed to the Treaty of New Echota. The agreement was to relinquish all the lands of the Cherokee east of the Mississippi, thus initiating the aforesaid Trail of Tears migration to Oklahoma. In Watie's view, the treaty offered the Cherokee people their best opportunity for an independent life going forward.

The treaty however was not approved by the ruling Cherokee National Council and, one year later, Watie's three relatives were murdered by their fellow tribesmen via the claim that they had violated their Blood Law.

By 1861, Waite had settled into the area of Honey Creek, Indian Territory - now Oklahoma. The Civil War had broken out and Watie, who saw the Union as the greater threat to the Cherokee than the Confederacy, raised a unit called the Mounted Cherokee Rifles. By all accounts, he proved himself to be a talented battlefield leader, both in the conventional and guerrilla aspects of the war.

In 1863, Watie was elevated to the rank of Brigadier General, commanding the First Indian Brigade of the Confederate Army of the Trans-Mississippi. Eventually, however he submitted to the inevitable on June 23, 1865 - two months after Appomattox. He ultimately returned to Honey Creek, where he was to die.

And so much for that.

One of Hawk's disenchanted cousins had once questioned why he had sought a career as an *ayosgi* - a soldier - in the very same Army that had once persecuted their ancestors.

"Not the same Army," Hawk replied. "And besides selling dope, what are you doing for our people?"

The cousin spat on the floor and walked out.

They never spoke again.

Hawk whispered a prayer for the sprits of the dead and returned to his car. His cousin was right in one sense. The past was never truly gone.

But his issues today were with the agents of the Islamic Republic - not those of the Jacksonian Republic.

Hawk finished his beer, climbed back into the driver's seat and headed out. There was more to be done.

= SIXTEEN =

DUNN LORING

Dunn Loring, Virginia
August 23, 2004

The small enclave of Dunn Loring is less a political entity and more of a postal address in Fairfax County, Virginia, adjacent to the affluent Tysons and McLean areas. It is the home of the Washington Field Office and of the Training Center of the State Department's Diplomatic Security Service. Both are co-located in an office park on Gallows Road, not far from Route 66 and the Capital Beltway.

It was a sleepy Monday morning. Leah Chaikin had been forewarned by her unit supervisor that she needed to stop in for a visit with the Special Agent in Charge of WFO before heading back south for a few more days at the ATF warehouse in North Carolina.

With one hand holding a coffee cup from the neighboring 7-Eleven convenience store and cradling a notebook with her elbow, she used her free hand to tap delicately on the door jamb of the SAC's office.

Jake Kaczmar, the SAC, glanced up over his glasses from his computer screen. "Leah," he said smiling. "Come on in. And close the door."

She dropped into a chair in front of his desk. "Bobby said that you needed to see me before I left," she said tentatively. As an untenured junior agent, she didn't know whether that was necessarily a good thing or a bad thing.

"Am I in trouble?" she asked.

"Hardly," the SAC replied.

Kaczmar pulled a folder off of the credenza behind him and opened it on his desktop. "Henry Bayard," he said, without introduction. "That name mean anything to you?"

She struggled briefly to scrounge up a bit of connected memory but quickly shook her head. "Uhm. Sorry. No."

"Yeah, he's not so well-known. Maybe a minor celebrity in the analytic community up the river," Kaczmar said. "He was an Air Force guy. Part of the Defense Attaché's Office in Beirut a few years back." He showed her an 8x10 photograph of Bayard standing alongside a few of his colleagues at some nondescript location.

"Looks nice enough," Leah ventured evenly.

"Oh yeah," the SAC agreed. "Very nice. Smart, quiet, dutiful. Kept to himself quite a bit."

He pushed a copy of an old news story from the Washington Post across the desk. "But in October of 1996, our boy went missing from the embassy."

"Eight years ago. Okay."

"Whether he was kidnapped, went AWOL, committed suicide, slipped and fell into the ocean, or was abducted by a UFO, nobody knew," Kaczmar said, continuing with his story. "But he was gone for sure, mysteriously, in a city well known for its kidnapping of Westerners."

"Okay," she repeated, wondering where this tale was headed and what it had to do with her.

"A month or so ago," he said, "your ATF pals were set up on that I-95 rest stop when Mutt and Jeff were making another tobacco smuggling run up to New York. That time they shot a few photos of a car that they assumed was covering the smugglers. As in providing a professionally trained counter-surveillance function."

"Yes," she agreed, well aware of that development in the case.

The SAC placed a remarkably clear, enlarged photo of the driver of the suspected counter-surveillance vehicle. "Remember that?"

"Sure," she said, glancing at it. "Freddy was happy to be able to start fleshing out the Hezbollah smuggling cell, based on this guy and two others at the check-cashing store in High Point. The ATF offices in New York and Charlotte are looking into all three of them right now."

"Let's save them some trouble," Kaczmar said. "On a hunch, our DS analysts in Rosslyn sent this photo downtown to the Consular Affairs people. CA ran it through the facial recognition program for passport and visa photos."

"Oh."

"As a tool, it's a bit new and they're still working out the kinks, but the software made a positive hit. It was linked to a tourist passport issued in 1999 in Santo Domingo for someone named Thomas William Adkins. White male. Born June 10, 1969, in Topeka, Kansas."

"Alright," Leah said, nodding. "Looking good for the home team."

Kaczmar held up a cautioning hand. "Except that, unfortunately, Tommy Adkins was killed in a boating accident in Missouri at the age of six."

"Dead baby birth certificate," Leah mused, catching up to the storyline.

"But that's not the best part," Kaczmar said, clearly relishing his story. "CA made a second facial recognition hit on the same photo. An earlier diplomatic passport bore the same identifiable photograph of a man named Henry Roger Bayard, born March 16, 1967 in Clovis, New Mexico."

"Bayard? Well, son of a bitch," Leach muttered quietly.

"Yeah," Kaczmar grinned. "Your guys appear to have found our missing Air Force sergeant."

Leah opened her notebook and began jotting down a few facts. "Okay to share this with ATF?"

"Yeah, sure," Kaczmar said. "No secrets here. About that anyway."

"Hmmm," she pondered aloud as she finished scribbling her notes. "Why the passport application in Santo Domingo? That's the Dominican Republic, right?"

"Correct," Kaczmar said. "State Department people always get top marks for geography. But to answer your question, and no doubt ATF's as well, the DR is a high-volume fraud post. The greater the percentage of fraudulent visa and passport applications that are made, the more likely that some will evade the filters. That's not a secret either."

"ATF's going to wet their pants when they hear this," Leah observed happily.

"Go get 'em Sport," Kaczmar said, dismissing her and turning his attention back to his computer screen. "And let's see where this goes."

= SEVENTEEN =

JADE SORCERER

McLean, Virginia
August 27, 2004

Angela arguably knew JD Tucker, the Org director, better than anyone else within the JICSA structure. As the house wags would have it, this included intimate knowledge in both the carnal as well as the psychological sense. And, although their supposedly off -the-record relationship was now consigned to the past, it was nevertheless true.

That being the case, she saw the signs of haggardness about Tucker's eyes as he entered the secure room. Meyerhof, the loyal deputy director, secured the heavy, soundproofed door behind the general and found his own seat alongside of him.

Angela and the other staff members were seated around the table in Conference A, the Headquarters' SCIF, or the Sensitive Compartmented Information Facility.

"Good morning, everyone," Tucker intoned. And a special welcome aboard to Lonnie Mills, our new ChiefOps."

The newcomer to the table was a powerfully built black man, newly arrived from the state of Florida. His title was Chief of Operations, or more simply as ChiefOps. Despite being selected for the new position several months earlier, after dealing with some recurring medical issues, this was actually his first appearance at a full staff meeting. "Thank you, sir," he replied with an engaging, political smile. "Very good to be here."

An Ocala native, Mills long ago won a football scholarship out of high school that took him up the road to join the Gators football team at the University of Florida. There, while he majored in criminology, his athletic star continued to shine.

Graduating from UF, Mills was drafted into the NFL as a running back for the Denver Broncos. Unfortunately, in one of his initial pre-season games, Mills exemplified the old bromide that, in the NFL, you are always just one play away from retirement.

In that one game, on a muggy Thursday night, Mills sprinted to the end zone and went up to catch a long Hail Mary pass from the quarterback. As he recalled, he had been under heavy coverage. He caught the pass but came down with a career-ending broken leg.

His brief football career suddenly over, Mills returned to Florida where he eventually became a local police officer. After a few years at the municipal level, he was accepted into the Florida Department of Law Enforcement as a Special Agent.

The FDLE is the state-wide criminal investigations and intelligence agency. By dint of his admitted sports popularity, as well as native talent, Mills steadily rose through the ranks of the FDLE, eventually becoming the Assistant Commissioner of Investigations. In that role, he oversaw seven regional operations centers and fourteen field offices.

And now he was with the JICSA crew.

Peering about at the dozen or so faces around the table, Tucker cleared his throat and began his part of the presentation. "Before we get started with today's agenda, let me address the situation up in the Baltics," he said, "which I know is an issue with many of you.

"The northern operation has now expanded across all three countries - Lithuania, Latvia and Estonia. The circumstances for our team on the ground are dicey. No denying that."

Mills scratched some notes on his pad. He was in catch-up mode, still just getting read in on the various Org projects around the world.

Tucker returned the concerned looks of his senior staff. "Although we have hit some unexpected roadblocks," he continued in a level tone of voice, "the operation is continuing as planned. We have asked State to intervene with the locals to try and slow down these actions of the Russian opposition. I still have high expectations of success."

He paused to take a sip of water. "So. Without going any further into the dirty details, that's where we stand with that case... Any questions? No? Good

"So, what's on the agenda this morning?"

"First up today is the Iranian account," Meyerhof chimed in to start the discussion. "As we all know, it appears that last May the MOIS took it upon itself to abduct a US intelligence officer, for reasons as of yet unknown. Wittingly or not, their operation caught one of our case officers in the crosshairs."

"And that individual would be Chalice," Tucker supplied, his cheeks slightly reddening. Clearly the incident was an issue of personal concern. "Who is still recovering from multiple gunshot wounds in a hospital in Birmingham, Alabama."

"Correct," Meyerhof said. "But some good news... One of the two bullets that hit Chalice bounced around internally after it landed. Caused some complications."

"That's the good news?" Tucker prodded.

"Good news is that the docs think they can discharge him in a few days. He'll need a little convalescent time though."

"Staying where?" Tucker asked. "Do we know?"

Meyerhof glanced at his notes. "Looks like with his daughter in Wilmington, Delaware. She's an RN now with the VA Medical Center there."

"That would be Tas," Angela reflected. Tas, or Tasanee, was Chalice's daughter with his Thai ex-wife, Somchai. Somchai was a beauty in her own right and the daughter of a former Thai general. Somchai and Chalice met and married during his Special Forces days, but the marriage was not to last.

Tas was an only child. Angela had seen earlier photos of her but had never met her in person. Hard to believe that she was now a grown woman.

"Good development," Tucker said. "But still, that shooting was an unacceptable aggressive action. A violation of protocol, regardless of who they thought he was. And I won't stand for it," Tucker glowered. "It is an offensive move that has to be answered. By us. Directly."

"Understood," Meyerhof agreed.

"So then, where are we on this?"

"ChiefOps," Meyerhof said, gratefully tossing it to the newly acquired Chief of Operations.

"Okay, the JADE SORCERER case," Mills began, slipping easily into the role. This was, he well knew, the first major case under his purview. "Having reviewed the file, I have to say that we're in a bit of luck here. It appears that our SORCERER case officer, Hawk, has already had past dealings with an individual who is again connected to the case."

"And by that you mean..." Tucker led.

"Henry Bayard," Mills said. "Native born American citizen. Former US Air Force NCO. Top Secret clearance. SCI access. Previously of the Defense Attaché Office at the Embassy in Beirut, Lebanon."

"And one of our formerly missing people," Meyerhof added.

"Yes sir," Mills agreed. "Who recently, and quite surprisingly, reappeared in High Point, North Carolina. Of all places in the world." He sat a pair of reading glasses on the bridge of his nose and began to page through a Moleskine notebook.

"As it develops," he continued. "Hawk was involved with the Bayard incident as far back as 1997. That was before his time with the Org when he was still in the Army's Intelligence Support Activity. The ISA.

"During that time, Hawk located a source in Beirut. That source led him to a man named Yaqub who may have been connected with Bayard's disappearance." He took a moment to consult his notes in greater detail.

"You are referring to that fellow in the Bekaa Valley," Angela prompted. "Which was what? Seven years ago?"

"Correct. This Yaqub has been confirmed as a local leader in the village of Nahleh," he continued. "That's in the Baalbek area. It's known for ancient Roman ruins, ancient Arab ruins... And the modern Hezbollah cronies of Iran."

"It also has a more contemporary history of hashish and opium cultivation," someone chimed in.

"Right again," Mills agreed. "Not a place with a strong history of law enforcement or legal compliance... And this is where Bayard appeared to have spent somewhere between one and two years after his unauthorized departure from the US Embassy. Based on allied information."

"Allied," Tucker interrupted. "Like who?"

"The Israelis," Mills answered, briefly removing his glasses. "Apparently after Hawk picked up on this lead, our friends in the Defense Department asked the Israelis to take a look. The Mossad tasked one of their local sources to visit the little burg of Nahleh."

"And?"

"The source positively identified the Yaqub figure not only as the village leader but also as a known Hezbollah activist. The source was also able to confirm that a male foreigner was living in the village under this Yaqub's protection. The foreigner was said to have been a convert to Islam who was there to study the Koran."

"And a little more besides that, I'm guessing" Meyerhof ventured.

"Did they confirm the identity of the foreigner?" Tucker asked.

Lonnie Mills shook his head. "No positive ID, but the physical description did generally fit that of Bayard."

He let that factoid settle in with the gathering for a few seconds.

"And so back to High Point, North Carolina," Angela added, joining the discussion. "ATF is doing a smuggling case down there. While running surveillance on the suspects, they snapped a good photo of a white guy who was sitting in a counter-surveillance, covering car at an I-95 rest stop." She passed a few blown-up copies of the black and white photo around the table.

"The Consular Affairs people at State just did a facial recognition match between old passport photos of Bayard and the one matching the individual in the car," she continued. "It is Bayard. They are 90 percent certain of it."

"Then I guess we can assume that Bayard has finished whatever training Hezbollah had in mind for him. And he is now operational. Back here in the US," Tucker concluded.

"That would be my guess," Mills agreed. "Although what else he might be up to is simply conjecture, at this point."

"If I may, let's switch from we *might* know to what we *do* know," another voice piped up. "We may be looking at this from the wrong end of the telescope."

Angela was surprised to see that was Landau weighing in, unsummoned.

"Okay Mister Landau," Tucker said, acknowledging the presence of their Iran analyst. "What'cha got?"

Landau started ticking off his points on his fingertips. "One. The Iranians came at us. No doubt of that.

"Two. Thanks to Hawk, it's obvious that this Bayard character has flipped. He is now an enemy agent. That makes him a legitimate target of ours. More to be learned about him at a later point.

"Three. Again, thanks to Hawk and our T/Pan proprietary company in Luxembourg, our main reach into the MOIS is now this Shahriar Parviz fellow. An up-and-comer in Tehran."

"Go on. I'm with you," Tucker said.

"But Parviz is just an up-and-comer," Landau explained. "He's not there yet. From all the reports I've seen, he has a big stumbling block standing in the way of his upward progression. And therefore, also someone in the way of our increased penetration."

"Who do you have in mind?"

"An official named Javed Mokri."

"And why him?" Mills challenged. "Whoever he is."

"He's a senior member of their Supreme National Security Council," Landau said. "Works directly under Hassan Rouhani, who is a real powerhouse in Iran. Frankly, I see Mokri as the next director of the MOIS."

"What do you know about him?" Tucker prompted.

Landau leaned forward on the table, flexing his shoulders as he typically did when preparing to drive home a cogent point. "He's a well-placed political operator with a good pedigree."

"Pedigree?" Tucker repeated. "Like what?"

Landau nodded. "Aside from his political work, he is also a Muslim cleric. He's a graduate of the Haqqani School in Qum, which is the center of Shi'ite religious studies. He has a Ph.D. in Islamic Studies."

"Significance?"

"Ever since the Ayatollah Khomeini established the post of MOIS director, each one of them has been a Doctor of Islam. To include the current director, someone named Younesi. He also has a Western-backed education, having once, as a younger guy, attended an elite school in France called Sciences Po, or the Paris Institute of Political Studies... Maybe something we can use there."

"Javed Mokri," Tucker reflected, savoring the name. "Sounds like a heavy hitter."

"He is," Landau said. "No doubt about it. He's your shot caller... He's your JADE SORCERER."

Tucker ruminated on that for a moment. "And maybe," he said. "A means of placing our fox in their henhouse."

= EIGHTEEN =

LIKE THE DEAD

Tehran, Iran
September 7, 2004

Javed Mokri grimaced as he read the report that had been delivered to his desk earlier that morning. It was delayed in its delivery, despite having been published a few months earlier. Only now had it belatedly come to the attention of the MOIS. And then the intelligence people forwarded it to him at the Supreme National Security Council, or SNSC.

Nevertheless, here it was. The article had been released by what he assumed to be the Zionist-leaning American group calling themselves Human Rights Watch. Its title was "Like the Dead in Their Coffins: Torture, Detention and the Crushing of Dissent in Iran." Grimacing, he had little doubt of the content that was to come.

The very first paragraph of the piece was enough to set his teeth on edge. "No one knows how many people are held in Iran's prisons and secret detention centers for the peaceful expression of their views." Mokri reflected that even he did not know that number. But he had a very good idea.

He paused to give thanks that the recent February elections had witnessed a victory of the conservative faction over the reformists in parliament. He knew the unspoken fact that the results were greatly aided by the disqualification of some 2,500 reformist candidates a month prior to the election.

"Over the past four years," the article continued, "as the window of free expression has closed in Iran, abuse and torture of dissidents have increased in Evin Prison's solitary cells and secret detention centers."

On the opposite wall of his office was the framed official portrait of the Supreme Leader, the Grand Ayatollah Ali Hosseini Khamenei. Gray-bearded, black-turbaned, and bespectacled, the visage of Khamenei returned his gaze ruefully. There was no doubt as to how Khamenei would respond to the article. He expected Mokri to do his duty. And so, he would.

Khamenei was only the second Supreme Leader in the brief history of the Islamic Republic. He was preceded in office by Ruhollah Khomeini, the man that most Americans thought of when they heard the term *Ayatollah*.

Returning to the article, he read the claim that there had been an unprecedented wave of newspaper closures since the year 2000. True enough, he thought, although he disagreed with the interpretation as a repression of free speech. In view of the threat of potential counter-revolutionaries, the actions of the government were more than justified.

The report paid special attention to the home of political enemies, Evin Prison, which it described as being in an eerily beautiful location for a prison. Accurately enough, Human Rights Watch attributed the founding of the prison not to the current regime, but to the late Shah's secret police, the SAVAK.

More surprisingly to Mokri, the report had information on the facility called Prison 59. Operated by the Islamic Revolutionary Guard Corps, 59 was more of a psychological punishment venue in which the inmates, largely dissident students and journalists, were subjected to long-term solitary confinement and enforced absolute silence.

The report cited a statement by the European Commission on Human Rights to the effect that "complete sensory isolation coupled with total social isolation, can destroy the personality and constitutes a form of treatment which cannot be justified by the requirements of security or any other reason."

Having been one of the intellectual founders of Prison 59, Mokri found a bit of satisfaction in the reported quote of a former inmate that he "...could not imagine spending one night in those solitary cells without losing my mind." Another stated, "After three days, I just wanted any words. Even if it was swearing, even if it was a harsh words interrogation."

Mokri flipped to a new page. "The word most commonly used by prisoners to describe the solitary cells," he read, "was coffin."

The piece concluded with the opinion that the outlook for Iran's future was bleak, with little hope for change in the behavior of the judiciary. Closing the report folder, Mokri recalled a quote by the American political scientist, Graham Allison, who was himself citing a Truman-era bureaucrat, to the effect that "where you stood depends on where you sat."

Mokri sat very near the center of power at the heart of the Islamic Republic of Iran.

He made a note to ensure that a Farsi translation was made of the article, which he would forward to his superior at the SNSC, Hassan Rouhani.

= NINETEEN =

DAY TRIPPER

US Attorney's Office
Greenbelt, Maryland
September 8, 2004

Located thirteen or so miles east of Washington, DC, is the city of Greenbelt, Maryland. It is situated in a wooded and deceptively remote area of the suburban Washington metroplex. Although it was a pleasant September day, it would not be long before the greenery surrendered to the brown and gray hues of the approaching winter months.

Despite its proximity to Washington, Greenbelt's location was comfortably removed from the prying foreign and public eyes of the immediate national capital area. Even better, from an operational viewpoint, it offered a federal office building. The structure in question housed the Office of the United States Attorney - Southern Division of the of District of Maryland.

Hawk eased his rental into the parking area and found a suitable space at the far end of the parking lot. Killing the engine, he slipped a compact Beretta pistol out of his waistband and tucked it under the driver's seat.

After locking and double-checking the doors, he started for the building, conscious that surveillance cameras were likely recording his movements even then. Although it was, to be sure, friendly territory, operational habits were woven into the fabric of his daily life by now. Cameras were inherently unfriendly in his experience.

Hawk entered the smallish lobby of the building and nodded to the guard. The latter peered at him from a ballistically protected booth. He gave the guard a name that matched the one on the Virginia driver's license that he presented though the document tray. Following a brief check of scheduled visitors, Hawk was given a temporary ID badge latched onto a beaded chain.

That done, he was instructed to take a seat and wait.

After another several long minutes of cooling his heels in the empty lobby, a young female intern appeared to greet him. Although she tried to mask it, Hawk could see that the intern, most likely a local college kid, was slightly taken aback by his somewhat intimidating, non-federal agent, appearance.

After verifying his ID, the intern led him through the hard line to a bank of elevators. At last, she escorted him to a secure conference room on one of the upper floors of the building. There she took her leave and did not seem unhappy to be doing so.

Three men were awaiting Hawk in the conference room. Of the trio, he recognized only one, and that was Lonnie Mills.

"Hawk," the ChiefOps said, rising to his feet and extending a hand. "Good to see you."

"Likewise, sir," Hawk replied, eyeing the other two men. He already knew that they would be representatives of the US State Department. He had been told that they had pertinent information to share. Information that was related to his case.

Mills identified the two State employees as Jake Kaczmar, the Special Agent in Charge of the Diplomatic Security Service's Washington Field Office, and Charlie Grant, a senior analyst with the DSS Office of Intelligence and Threat Analysis, or ITA.

They were a contrasting pair. The SAC was a large, buff and ruddy figure. The DS/ITA analyst, on the other hand, was a thin, white-haired man with piercing blue eyes and a keen professorial demeanor.

All nodded agreeably, shook hands, and took their seats about the freshly polished tabletop.

"Gentlemen, this is Hawk," Mills told the State people by way of introduction as they settled back into their chairs. "He is one of our JICSA case officers. Hawk has a long history of covert operations abroad. Both with the Org and with the Army's Intelligence Support Activity."

Head nods and expressions of fraternal understanding were exchanged amiably. Until a few days earlier however, the State Department people had never heard of JICSA. Signed non-disclosure agreements soon followed to ensure their future silence on the matter.

"What our State colleagues have," Mills began, turning the conversation back to Hawk's direction, "is some pertinent information regarding one of the subjects of your JADE SORCERER case."

"Glad to have it," Hawk said. "Anything to get some more traction on this."

"And by some strange coincidence," Mills continued, "it also involves someone from your past life. That is to say, your life back in the ISA."

"Okay. I'm waiting," Hawk quipped during the pause.

"It's someone called Henry Bayard... Recognize the name?"

Initially, Hawk did not.

"Hank Bayard," Charlie Grant, the DSS analyst prompted. "Defense Attaché Office. Beirut, Lebanon."

"Bayard," Hawk mused momentarily as the reflections slowly came to him. "Was that the Air Force DAO guy who went missing in Beirut?"

"The very same," Grant affirmed.

"They never heard from him, or of him, again," Hawk said. "That must have been in nineteen, uh..."

"Nineteen Ninety-Seven," Mills completed the thought.

"Alright. I remember him. Now missing for about seven years or so then," Hawk observed. "Dead, as far as I know."

"Missing until now," Grant said. "We think that your old Beirut target is still very much alive and well. And still in the game."

"But playing for the other side these days," Kaczmar added.

Hawk leaned forward and clasped his hands on the buffed conference table. "Where is he... These days?"

"Most recently seen in the town of High Point," Kaczmar answered. "North Carolina. The United States of America."

Hawk arched his eyebrows quizzically.

"Bayard recently surfaced as part of an on-going joint undercover case that we have with ATF down in North Carolina," Kaczmar continued. "The case is called DAY TRIPPER. Numerous federal charges are pending. Tobacco smuggling. Fraudulent documents. Tax evasion. Probably weapons charges as well, before it's all over."

"And ties with Hezbollah," Grant added.

"And Hezbollah means Iran," Kaczmar said. "Credible sources claim that Iran is funding Hezbollah to the tune of some $100 to $200 million dollars per year. Some of that is in cash, the rest of it in weapons and other logistic support."

"The hardware being off-loaded in Syria and then trucked overland to the camps in the Bekaa Valley," Grant added.

"Our State friends tell me that Hezbollah is surprisingly active right here in the US as well," Mills commented to Hawk.

Kaczmar nodded. "That group seems to be the movers and shakers behind this scheme. Not surprisingly, it appears that all of the profits generated here in the United

States by this group are being channeled straight back to their home station in Lebanon."

"Correct," Grant said, taking up the lead. "Hezbollah has a number of operations here - primarily in North Carolina, New York, Michigan, and California. The majority of them are involved in money laundering and the smuggling of various goods. Others are doing weapons procurement, developing recruits to travel to the Mideast, or doing pre-operational surveillance of potential terror targets."

Not all of this was new information to Hawk. "How does Bayard figure into this?" he asked the DSS SAC. "In North Carolina?"

Kaczmar deferred to Grant. "You go ahead," he said.

"North Carolina," Grant continued. "Charlotte in particular is very important to Hezbollah. It seems that there are two brothers there, the Hamouds, who report directly to a Hezbollah military commander in South Beirut named Sheikh Fadlallah. He's on Treasury's list of Specially Designated Terrorists, by the way."

"To us," Grant said, pursuing the narrative, "it looks like Bayard may have been doing no more than a guest appearance in the North Carolina smuggling case."

"A guest appearance?" Mills repeated.

"Yes. Well, we know that he traveled up there on a false identity," Grant said.

"As in using an American passport that was issued in the name of someone named Thomas Adkins," Kaczmar interjected. "Actually, Adkins is the true identity of a dead American citizen. Unofficially, it's what we call a dead baby ID. The identity of a dead infant or a fairly young minor."

"A dead infant?" said Hawk. "That didn't ring any bells?"

"Correct," Kaczmar replied. "That's an unfortunate part of our system... To date, there is no system of tracking or linking between the birth records and death records of US citizens. That being the case, it's fairly easy for a foreigner to claim citizenship of a deceased American fitting their age and ethnicity and slip in through the cracks."

Hawk shifted position in the hard, wooden chair as he absorbed this information. "You say he traveled to North Carolina on the Adkins passport... From where?" he asked. "Lebanon?"

"That's the interesting part," Grant supplied. "He came in from the TBA. Specifically, Paraguay."

Hawk traded a brief glance with ChiefOps and shook his head. "TBA? Means nothing to me," he said.

Mills shrugged his shoulders in agreement.

"Sorry," Grant said. "The region itself is called the TBA. Otherwise known as the Tri-Border Area."

The analyst paused to unfold a map sheet onto the tabletop. He pushed it across toward Hawk and the ChiefOps.

"The TBA," Grant continued, "describes a point in South America where the national borders of Argentina, Paraguay, and Brazil all converge. It has a well-deserved reputation of being a fairly lawless, Wild West kind of area. Hezbollah, among other groups, has been free to operate there and generate profits for the folks back home."

Hezbollah, he went on to explain, was only one of several extremist groups that were welcomed, or at least operationally uninhibited, within the TBA region. The others included such global bad actors as Hamas, al-Qaeda, al-Islamiyah, al-Jihad, and several others.

Between them, and others who were not so politically inclined, the various entities were active in a wide variety of criminal activities. Whatever venture that promised to make money was as good as any other, as it seemed.

"The totality of criminal incidents in the TBA are incalculable," Kaczmar said, pulling an unclassified document out of a folder and sliding it over to the JICSA team.

"Doing what, in general?" the ChiefOps asked as Hawk thumbed through the DSS report.

"You name it, they do it," Kaczmar replied. "Criminal financing, tax evasion, money moving, terrorist bombings, killings, trafficking in people, guns and drugs, violations of intellectual property rights. They do it all."

"A real-life den of thieves then," Mills reflected, glancing at the document in Hawk's hands.

"A murderous den of thieves," Grant agreed. "At the very least."

"Do we know where Bayard is in the TBA?" Hawk asked.

"Yes, we do. He's in Ciudad del Este. It's a Paraguayan city on the border with Brazil."

"And Bayard's role in all of this?" Hawk asked.

"From our friends in Treasury, especially FinCEN," Grant replied, "it looks like Bayard may now be one of Hezbollah's prime money handlers in the TBA. As I'm sure you know, none of these activities can survive without reliable and regular monetary infusions. It's their lifeblood."

FinCEN, or the Financial Crimes Enforcement Network, was the unit of the US Treasury that collected intelligence on terrorist financing and other financial crimes. It was located in Vienna, Virginia, not all that far from the JICSA headquarters itself. It was the US Government entity that really did follow the money.

Mills turned his attention Hawk. "Bayard," he said. "You think he might be another way into JADE SORCERER?"

"Could be," Hawk said, rolling up the DSS report in his hands. "You don't know if you don't ask."

= TWENTY =

SNATCH

Nahle, Lebanon
September 16, 2004

It was just before three in the morning, local time, in Lebanon.

Two pairs of specially equipped Blackhawk helicopters whispered in through the night over the edge of the Lebanese border. They came in low, skirting over the surface of the Mediterranean, on a steady easterly heading. The helos began kicking up vaporous swirlings of loose sand in their trail as they cleared the *wet foot/dry foot* littoral line.

The first pair of Blackhawks were troop carriers, each transporting teams of hardened and heavily armed US Army Delta Force assaulters. The second pair were along to serve the twin purpose of suppressive fire gunships and as spare troop carriers, should the need for either purpose arise.

All four were crewed by members of the Army's 160th Special Operations Aviation Regiment - otherwise known as the Night Stalkers.

Their joint target that night was a house that was located on the far northern outskirts of the Lebanese village of Nahle. Assuming that the intel was accurate, inside that structure was an elderly man named Yaqub Khadim Ghaziri.

According to the operational briefing, despite his rustic surroundings, the target had emerged as a trusted financial operative in the Hezbollah network. Someone back home dearly wanted to get him under control for reasons unknown and entirely irrelevant to the members of the Delta team.

One way or another, Ghaziri's life was about to change forever.

On board the lead aircraft, making his unrelenting way toward Yaqub Ghaziri, was the Delta team leader, an Army Captain whose call sign was Triton.

Triton had been an aficionado of the classics, prior to his attraction to the military life. After being assigned the mission, he researched the target area. As an aside, he learned that the ruins of an ancient Roman temple were within the village of Nahle. The structure, supposedly more than a thousand years old, was part of a series of ruins that were dotted along the Bekaa Valley. All was courtesy of the Roman Legions who occupied what was then Phoenicia.

His personal interests aside, the parameters of the mission would not enable Triton to see the ruins on this particular night.

So near yet so far.

"Twelve minutes out," came the voice of the command pilot in his headphones. "Copy?"

"Twelve mikes... Roger that," Triton replied softly, refocusing on the task at hand.

Although the Blackhawks were quickly closing in on the target, another American airframe was already there ahead of them.

The early intruder took the form of an unarmed, remotely piloted Global Hawk drone. Even then, it was orbiting silently overhead of the village, monitoring it in the stillness of the night.

The man controlling the Global Hawk drone from afar was a US Air Force officer named Jimenez. He was sitting at a workstation that was more than seven thousand miles and ten time zones to the west of the village.

Specifically, Jimenez was located at a facility called Indian Springs. It was situated in the state of Nevada, between Nellis Air Force Base and the city of Las Vegas.

The Global Hawk drone, with its night vision optics, was sending back images of a quiet, sleepy village from Lebanon to Nevada. All was as hoped and expected on the ground.

As Jimenez peered at the screen, the speaker next to it came to life.

"Ajax, Ajax," a tinny voice echoed from out of the ethers. "This is Triton... How copy? Over."

"Triton, this is Ajax," Jimenez immediately replied. "Good copy. Go with your traffic. Over."

"SitRep? Over."

"All is looking good on your end," the Air Force officer answered. "Everything is nominal for the mission. Over."

"Much thanks," Triton responded. "Now at Phase Two. Over."

"Copy Phase Two," Jimenez said. "Standing by."

"Roger... Triton out."

* * *

In his experience, Jimenez was never alone in his controller booth while in the course of an active mission. That afternoon was no different. A Delta liaison officer from Fort Bragg was sitting in the chair right next to him. The visitor was tightly focused on the black and white screens before them. The coffee in the mug at his side was rapidly cooling, unnoticed.

As they watched, the speaker came to life once again. "Ajax, this is Triton," called the voice. "Now signal Phase Three. Over."

By his declaration, the troop-carrying Blackhawks were then on the ground in Lebanon, yet still some distance from the target village of Nahle. The two support ships remained airborne a few miles offset from Triton's position.

"Copy Phase Three," Jimenez replied. "Your status remains in the green. Both above and below."

The Delta liaison officer nodded to him and then took control of the mic. "Triton, this is Ajax-Able," he said. "You are cleared to execute. On your command. Copy? Over."

"Understood," the team leader in Lebanon answered flatly. "Triton out."

On the ground, the team leader waited until the helicopters had lifted off and retreated to their predesignated hide site. "Okay, listen up," he called quietly over the intra-team radio net to the rest of the shooters. "Strobes on now. Let's move."

One by one the tiny infrared strobe lights mounted atop of their helmets flickered on. While invisible to the unaided eye, they were clearly detectable by the lens of the Global Hawk that continued to loiter overhead.

Satisfied with the imagery he was seeing, the Air Force officer tapped a message into the keyboard, directing the drone to re-route, moving it further eastward to return to its position above Nahle.

Outside of the Indian Springs UAV control bunker, the late afternoon traffic, both military and civilian, was making its way off of the base and heading home to their families. Or to wherever. The hodgepodge of commuters, one and all, were oblivious to the drama being played out in the inconspicuous building to the far side of their roadway.

* * *

It took nearly another half hour before the drone again visually reacquired the Delta team members. Their ghostly figures emerged from the periphery of its view. As it watched, they crept in on foot from the site of their initial landing zone. All the better to achieve the all-important element of surprise.

The team members paused on the far outskirts of the village for final coordination check. Satisfied, they fanned out into their assigned assault positions.

"Ajax, Triton... Signal Irish. Copy?"

The team leader was ready to hit the house.

"Copy Irish," Jimenez replied. "No human activity on site... One animal moving though. Looks like a dog. Or a wolf."

As the team closed in on the target house, a large stray dog appeared from the shadows whimpering at them. Annoyed at their unexpected approach, the animal barked once. Then twice.

A single suppressed rifle shot from one of the Delta operators caught the dog in its head and dropped it in its tracks.

"All clear," the team leader called. "Moving. Out."

"We copy," Jimenez replied.

As Jimenez and the Delta liaison watched, the imagery-enhanced figures of the team surrounded the target house. Upon Triton's signal, they made entry.

All was silent from the electronic perspective of Indian Springs, Nevada as the action took place in the Nahle village.

For the next few minutes Jimenez and the Delta liaison had nothing to do but to exchange tense glances.

The Delta liaison , Ajax-Able, took a brief sip of the cold coffee in his cup. "This is taking a while," he muttered, despite himself.

Finally, the audio feed came alive once again with its ghostly imagery. "Ajax, Triton. Now El Dorado," came the tinny voice. "I say again, El Dorado. You copy?"

The team leader was reporting that Yaqub Ghaziri was in custody. The team was moving to their pick-up point. No casualties.

“Good copy Triton,” the Delta liaison replied. “Good job. Stand by for extraction.”

The two officers in the Nevada location exchanged satisfied nods and a handshake.

A mission well done.

= TWENTY-ONE =

LINKAGE

September 24, 2004
McLean, Virginia

The core management group, minus the Director, settled into their usual chairs around the table. They were in the brightly lit SCIF of JICSA headquarters. As it was late on a Friday afternoon, all concerned were more than eager to get on with it and then go home for the weekend.

Kurt Meyerhof, the Deputy Director of JICSA, wearily opened the proceedings. "Okay everyone. I know it's been a long day and a long week," he said. "But there is one more thing on the agenda before we wrap it up."

He pushed a folder onto the tabletop. The folder bore a white cover sheet with a broken blue border on all four sides. It was labeled *Top Secret/HCS* - the HCS standing for *HUMINT Control System*, indicating the need for special handling of the already sensitive material contained therein. Meyerhof opened the cover and scanned the already familiar text on the facing page.

"JADE SORCERER," Meyerhof said. "Where do we stand on this?"

ChiefOps Lonnie Mills leaned forward in his seat. "Complicated case," he said. "With several moving pieces in play."

"To start with, the fellow in South America," Meyerhof offered. "There's something new on him? Yes?"

"Bayard," Mills said. "Correct."

"So?"

"As you know, Hawk and I met with some Diplomatic Security people in Greenbelt a week or so ago," the ChiefOps said. "Thanks to our friends at State, it looks like we may have pinned him down."

"Pinned him down. As in where?"

Angela took up the narrative. "The local police in Paraguay are pretty confident that they have located Bayard, thanks to help from facial recognition software."

"So where is Hawk's old friend now?"

Angela didn't need to refer to her notes. "A place called Ciudad del Este. It's a town in the so-called Tri-Border Area that encompasses Paraguay, Brazil and Argentina. He's now a convert to Islam. Currently married and goes by the name of Anas al-Kitaab. Also known as *Abu Saif."*

"Father of the Sword," Mills supplied. "From what they tell me, the TBA is a Wild West kind of area. All kinds of ethnic and religious groups there. A lot of free-wheeling operations underway. Not a lot of governmental control."

Meyerhof frowned. "So, a good area to house drug smugglers."

"Or terrorists," Mills added. "Or fugitives."

The JICSA Deputy settled back into his chair. "And just what does our Abu Saif do there in Ciudad del Whatever?"

"I guess you could say that he is dual-hatted," Angela said. "Bayard - if he really is this al-Kitaab figure - operates a small electronics sales and repair shop. With the help of his loving wife."

"But the PNP - the local cops - think that his real income comes from his business as a money mover," ChiefOps said, continuing the story. "Word is that he's linked into the hawala system, pushing money from the TBA to the Mid-East."

"Or money-laundering," Meyerhof suggested.

"Could be."

"Ideas?"

"Well, there's this," Mills began. "The established target of this operation is Javed Mokri... Now that we've tapped into the likely location of Bayard, let's leverage him against Mokri."

"I'm listening," Meyerhof said, visibly more alert than moments before.

"As we know, Mokri is a well-placed member of Iran's Supreme National Security Council," Mills said. "And, according to Landau's analysis, he could very well be the next head of their intelligence service."

"And so?"

"And so, what if he was revealed to be a spy for the Israelis?" ChiefOps posed. "What greater political disaster could there be for the Iranian regime?"

Meyerhof looked perplexed. "Is he?"

"No reason for us to think so," Mills admitted, raising his hands. "But he could be made to appear so."

Meyerhof frowned in concentration. "And just how would we go about darkening the reputation of this otherwise fine and loyal Iranian civil servant?"

"Money going into a private account," Mills said. "Like that coming from a foreign money launderer. Maybe one in far-off Paraguay."

"What we are thinking," said Angela, "is that there must be a way to tie Bayard into this. Let's say that the Org sets up an offshore account connected to Mokri. Maybe in Luxembourg, for example."

"Which is no stranger to the money laundering trade," Mills added. "And where we have Hawk's Technologie Pan front company, already established."

"Right," Angela continued. "And let's say that the Luxembourg account is linked to a numbered Swiss account. One that possibly can be run back to Mokri."

"And that such an account, previously connected with Israeli intelligence, is known to the Iranians to have been blown," said Mills.

"Is there such an account?" Meyerhof asked, now more interested.

"Don't know," Angela admitted. "But if there is such an account, NSA can find it for us."

"Let's surmise that there is such a blown account out there in the ethers," Meyerhof said. "Then what?"

"Well," Mills said, shaking his head. "It could be an opportunity for our guy Parviz to exploit. He gets to stab his enemy in the back and maybe move up a notch."

"And we get an agent in the upper reaches of the Iranian government," Meyerhof concluded.

"Could work," Mills said. "Worth a shot."

The JICSA Deputy Director jotted a note into the HCS folder. "Okay. Give it a try."

= TWENTY-TWO =

FACILITY BAR'AM

Bar'am, Israel
September 26, 2004

Early on the morning of September 25th, Yaqub Ghaziri broke from a troubled sleep. He was in a small chamber that had become depressingly ever more familiar to him. It was nothing like his home in Nahle, modest as it was.

His surroundings were roughly four feet by four feet square, with rough concrete all around and no padding on the floor. The dimensions allowed him neither to stretch out flat nor to stand up straight. A cramped posture in any direction was the only possibility.

The physical discomfort was very much by design.

It was the beginning of his tenth day in the enclosure. He had awoken on the first day after having been sedated by his kidnappers. The remaining days had increasingly blurred into a maze of confusion and discomfort.

As always, an empty coffee can rested in the corner of his constricted cell. It was, as he was told at the beginning, the only place where he could relieve himself when the urge to urinate came.

And the urge came frequently, since he was repeatedly forced to drink dog bowl sized containers of iced water. Before long, the can overflowed with urine, repeatedly wetting the floor of his cell. And the thin fabric of his pajama-like trousers.

When it did, Yaqub was pulled out of his cell and punished for his indiscretion with vigorous slaps to his head and torso, accompanied with loud verbal harangues. These were often delivered while he was placed into uncomfortable physical stress positions, such as leaning in a modified pushup configuration against an external wall for several hours.

Between the water treatments and the fierce admonishments from his captors, Yaqub was subjected to lengthy blasts of discordant music designed to keep him from sleep. From time to time the musical interludes were interrupted with eerie ramblings of a seemingly mad man who was endlessly holding forth in a barely discernible foreign language. And another of a small child who seemed to be repeatedly crying out for help.

Every so often, he eventually lost count, Yaqub was pulled from his cell and taken to a nearby interrogation room. There he was repeatedly asked about his connections to Hezbollah. Initially, he held firm. He denied all and everything. However, as the hours and days began to meld together his sense of clarity and persuasions began to crumble.

Combined with his hunger and programmed weariness, his hold on his convictions began to slip. He was not a young man. And slowly he began to talk. Haltingly but surely.

As heroically as he tried, Yaqub was increasingly having difficulty in denying his role in the Lebanese Hezbollah network. Despite his low profile, he was, in truth, a key financial intermediary in the Bekaa Valley.

As the days of interrogation continued, the questions began to shift from his operations in the Bekaa and more on the Israelis' apparent knowledge of his direct ties to the Hezbollah backers in Tehran.

Wearied as he was, Yaqub consciously locked onto a series of questions by his captors that struck even his troubled senses as odd in the extreme.

They wanted to know if he had heard rumors of a foreign agent serving the hierarchy of the MOIS in Tehran. When one of the questioners mentioned a possible Israeli source in the Iranian capital, he was unceremoniously pulled from the room by a senior officer and audibly chastised for his indiscretion.

While Yaqub denied any such knowledge, in truth he had encountered such a rumor before. Ironically, he overheard such a rumor days earlier from another set of Israeli guards who were speculating out of his hearing range. Or so they thought.

Still, the matter seemed odd to Yaqub's ears. It was a nugget of his imprisonment to remember. And to pass along when the time came.

* * *

Despite the length of his internment, Yaqub still had no clear idea as to his true physical location. In actuality, he had been held very closely to the border of Lebanon. The location was in a small facility on the outskirts of the kibbutz of Bar'am in the far northern reaches of Israel.

Bar'am was the site of an ancient Jewish settlement and synagogue called Kafr Bar'am, the ruins of which still existed. Yaqub was ignorant of the site and unlikely to ever tour the site in any event.

More importantly, adjacent to Bar'am was a small facility that was operated by the Israeli *Shin Bet*. As the Security Agency, also known as *Shabak*, Shin Bet was the domestic Israeli intelligence and security establishment. It was the twin sister of the *Mossad*, which was the more celebrated foreign intelligence service.

When the Org offered Shin Bet an opportunity to participate in an operation targeted against Hezbollah, they were more than happy to oblige.

* * *

Zev, a military veteran and the on-site Shin Bet supervisor, was perched behind a one-way mirror. He waited until Yaqub had reached the limits of what could be considered yet another fruitful session.

"Okay. That's enough," he said into a microphone. "Take him back to his cell."

The two men in the interrogation room nodded in response to the voice in their earpieces.

As Zev watched the images of the prisoner being removed on his TV screen, a blonde and bearded American loomed up alongside of him.

"Okay. What do you think?" Bear asked.

Bear had been at Bar'am since the beginning of the operation. He was serving as the Org's liaison to the Israelis for this phase. "It's been about two weeks now."

"We probably have as much out of him as we are going to get," the Israeli answered. "Unless we are willing to ramp up the physical pressure a bit... More than a bit... I'd say *quite* a bit."

Bear nodded. "That's the threat, isn't it?"

"Well, I think the seed has been planted," Zev said, hitching up his belt as he climbed out of his swivel chair. "Probably time to move him to Haifa."

"Sounds good," Bear smiled. "To Haifa then."

* * *

The next evening, a distraught Yaqub, fully hooded and shackled, was placed in the rear seat of a Toyota sedan. From the muted responses of his captors, he understood that his destination was the even harsher environment of a prison in Haifa. The ominous medieval citadel occupied an outcropping of land between Beirut and Tel Aviv.

Yaqub struggled to gather his sullen thoughts as the car began to move. Escape was impossible, insofar as he could determine. Continued resistance was unlikely. Still, agreeing to cooperate with the hated Israelis was more than he or his family could countenance, should they ever learn the truth.

Leaving his bleak fate to Allah seemed to be the only option for preserving his sanity, such as it was. And therefore, so be it.

Satisfied with his decision, he mumbled a quiet prayer for his salvation and settled back into his seat.

Some twenty minutes down the road Yaqub, still blind to his surroundings, felt the vehicle shudder violently as the driver abruptly hit the brakes. The familiar voices of his captors shouted to each other in alarm. While Yaqub could not understand Hebrew, he knew the sound of fear when he heard it.

Almost at once, he heard the blast of an explosion, slightly muffled by his thick hood. Several bursts of gunfire followed, accompanied by the sounds of shattering glass. The vehicle jolted violently as it hit a rut on the side of the road and came to a stop.

There was a moment of stunned silence until the rear door of the Toyota was pulled open with a screech of metal against metal. A hand grabbed Yaqub by his collar and roughly yanked him out of his seat.

"Out! Out now!" a male voice commanded him in Arabic. "Hurry old man! If you want to live!"

Although he could not see his surroundings, a pair of masked men hustled him away from the Toyota and tossed him bodily into the bed of an awaiting pick-up truck. One of the men clambered in beside him. Both were covered with a foul-smelling canvas tarp just before the truck accelerated away from the ambush site.

Given the proximity of the border, it took only several minutes until he was spirited back across the boundary into southern Lebanon. In less than an hour he was physically transferred to a Hezbollah intermediary who continued the task of returning Yaqub to his family and comrades.

He was free, but he retained his memories of captivity and his thoughts of vengeance.

Although Yaqub Ghaziri had no way of knowing it, his supposed "rescuers" were, in fact, covert members of the Israeli military. They belonged to Unit 217, also known as *Duvdevan*, the Hebrew word for Cherry. The soldiers of *Duvdevan* specialized in undercover operations in which they often passed themselves off as members of the Arab community.

Their role in the deception completed, the men returned to the safety of northern Israel.

And Bear returned to the States.

= TWENTY-THREE =

WIZARDRY

Off-Site Location
St. Michaels, Maryland
October 4, 2004

St. Michaels is a small town on the Eastern Shore of Maryland. Founded in the late 1600s, and named for an Anglican church, it is some 80 miles distant and a two-hours' drive east of Washington, DC. Throughout its long history, the town had been primarily known for shipbuilding, the harvesting of oysters and crabs, and, still later, tourism.

The town's historical claim to fame was that it served as the site of a small engagement during the War of 1812. The action has since been generously known as The Battle of St. Michaels.

In August of 1813, several British barges, essentially flat-bottomed boats propelled by oars, entered the Miles River from the Chesapeake Bay. They were intent on assaulting the town's fortifications and shipbuilding facilities.

Upon their arrival, the British bombarded the town with several rounds of cannon fire in an attempt to suppress any local resistance. The American defenders pulled back in response, allowing the Redcoats to safely land a number of lightly armed infantrymen.

As the Redcoats began to advance inland, an American battery opened fire on them. The unexpected action drove the Brits back to their barges, causing an ignominious retreat back up the river and into the bay. Although casualties were minimal, the event went down in the local lore as a great victory for the Americans.

And now, in the early days of fall, St. Michaels was the location of another off-site meeting of the Wizards.

The Wizards was a group of four carefully selected men, all of whom were retired senior officials of various agencies of the federal government. They served as a non-attributable oversight body for JICSA, the Org. As such, they formed a veneer of separation, however thin, between the Org and its true masters in the National Security Council.

As was their practice, the Wizards held their ad hoc meetings outside of the immediate DC area. Most often, this took place at locales offering a bit of sightseeing to accompany their often lethal deliberations.

On this occasion, the Wizards had convened with JD Tucker and Bart Landau at an elegant wood-frame house on Grace Street, a few blocks away from the marina on the Miles River. As was the standard practice, the structure had been previously swept by an Org technical team for electronic threats and was watchfully secured by inobtrusive armed sentries thereafter.

Anthony Wardlaw was one of the Wizards. He was a burly black man with a balding head, long sideburns and a full mustache. He retrieved two mugs of tea from the counter and carried them back to the table. A former career Foreign Service Officer, Wardlaw had been the Deputy Chief of Mission and then Ambassador to a number of US Embassies in Central America and Africa prior to his retirement from the State Department.

“Thanks,” the silver-haired Richard Kaufman muttered absently, accepting the mug of tea. He was peering intently at a file on the tabletop. A former attorney in the Office of the General Counsel at the National Security Agency, he tended to take the details of these operations a bit more granularly than the others.

"And so," Adolfo Torres said, impatiently addressing JD Tucker. "Our leader? Where could he be?"

"He's late, Adolfo," Tucker said, stating the obvious. The Org Director felt a degree of kinship with the single Hispanic member of the Org. Both were retired brigadier generals of the US Army. Tucker culminated his career as a special operator and commander with Delta, while Torres had been a long-term officer with Military Intelligence.

On the other side of the room, Bart Landau sat on a couch, rummaging through his briefing documents. He would be the presenter of the day. It would be his first interaction with the Wizards. Ignoring the banter of the others, he leafed through his notes, emphasizing the relevant portions with a yellow highlighter.

"News from Iraq is bad," Torres continued. "Fresh car bombings in Baghdad and Mosul. Twenty-six or so killed today."

"And we're still fighting to retake Fallujah," Wardlaw offered.

The observation hung in the air momentarily.

"JD?" Torres said. "So, Iraq this time?"

Tucker shook his head. "No sir. This has nothing to do with Iraq."

"Well, good then."

Several minutes later, a hand-held radio on the tabletop crackled with a single word from a member of the external security team.

"Arrival."

In short order the front door opened and the trim form of their Chairman, Barry Duguid, entered. "My apologies," the former CIA case officer and Clandestine Services executive exclaimed. "I came in late last night and went for a long run along the river this morning. A little too long, I guess. Showered up and here I am."

"No worries," Wardlaw said. "More than I could do."

"Appreciate it and good to see you all again," Duguid said, dropping into a chair at the table. He nodded, gratefully accepting a mug of black coffee. "I understand that Mister Landau has the floor this morning."

"That I do, sir," Landau said, approaching the table and distributing a classified handout to each of the Wizards. "The case of concern today, as I'm sure you are all aware, is called JADE SORCERER. Or, to clarify, the next step in the operation."

"What's the scope of this operation?" Duguid asked.

"Pretty wide-ranging , sir," Landau said. "It covers a false flag operation in Europe, a joint case with ATF and the State Department in North Carolina, and money launders in Lebanon and South America."

"And the main target is...?"

"A top figure in the Iranian intelligence service," Landau answered. "Maybe its next director."

Duguid smiled. "Okay. Let's hear it then."

= TWENTY-FOUR =

THE DARK TRIAD

McLean, Virginia
October 6, 2004

It was Wednesday, following the operations briefing to the Wizards. Bart Landau was back in his Org office, trying to catch up on pending business. Returning to his normal set routine, he fetched himself a mug of coffee from the break room and settled down to work.

Although the name of Henry Bayard was never mentioned at St. Michaels in connection with JADE SORCERER, the Air Force defector was in the forefront of Landau's mind now. This was especially true with regard to a collection of CIA assessment documents that were awaiting him in his in-box.

The topic of the documents was a CIA study of the causes of espionage. *Presumably,* Landau thought wryly, *the question was why our people spy for them. Not necessarily why the same types of people in their camp spy for us.*

Nevertheless, he was aware of a number of cases, especially of the Soviet era, when Bloc officers volunteered to provide information to CIA, MI6, and other Western agencies. Several even refused payment for their perilous services. These were described as examples altruistic or self-sacrificing motivations.

The CIA study, called PROJECT SLAMMER, was motivated by the upswing of cases involving cleared

Americans who decided to spy on behalf of various foreign powers in the period of the 1980s. This was specifically the case in 1985, the so-called Year of the Spy. That was the year that five security cleared Americans were caught spying for foreign entities.

These notorious five were Jonathan Jay Pollard, a US Navy Analyst who spied for Israel, John Anthony Walker, a US Navy warrant officer who spied for the Soviet Union, Reginald William Pelton, an NSA Commo Specialist who also spied for the Soviet Union, Larry Wu-Tai Chin, a CIA Linguist who spied for China, and, finally, Sharon Maria Scranage, a CIA stenographer who spied for Ghana.

The very iteration of their names reminded Landau of an article he once read claiming that a person's middle name was noted only after they became well known for notorious reasons. For example, the article claimed, neither John Wilkes Booth, Lee Harvey Oswald, nor John Wayne Gacy, among others, was ever known as such prior to the commission of their famous crimes. An interesting historical quirk, he thought.

Landau wondered, if the Org should start referring to their SORCERER subsidiary target as Henry Alan Bayard.

An FBI companion piece noted that the 1980s could also be called the Decade of the Spies, pointing out that many more than those five alone were caught, noting that 12 such individuals were found in the year 1984 alone. CIA's SLAMMER itself studied a total of 25 people, all male, who had decided to engage in espionage against the United States for one reason or another. Or, more accurately, for a compendium of reasons.

But why was this happening?

One of the documents in front of him was entitled The Dark Triad.-The study had been developed by a pair of Canadian psychologists named Paulhus and Williams. Their theory described the combined traits of narcissism (someone deserving of special treatment), psychopathy (a skilled manipulator, callous, unwilling to follow the rules, superficially charming), and Machiavellianism (believing that the ends justify the means) as being contributing factors to criminal episodes or other risk-taking behaviors of certain people.

Like committing espionage.

Like Henry Alan Bayard.

Maybe.

Via SLAMMER, CIA management tasked their psychologists to come up with a series of red-light issues that could be highlighted in terms of potential future security risks. One of their findings was what they called a critical pathway toward becoming a security risk. These include the personal predispositions of the individual stressors impacting their lives and concerning behaviors that they exhibited. All of these were compounded by what was termed maladaptive responses on behalf of their employing organizations.

The two other documents on his desktop paired the SLAMMER report findings with the Org-sponsored psych analysis of Bayard himself.

Essentially, the CIA team found that spies, like criminals - other criminals that was, tended to share certain motivations, driven by situational stressors and distorted patterns of thinking.

Landau turned his attention to the other two documents on his desk. To the left was the CIA report. To the right was the synopsis of the Org's analytical workup on Bayard's personality. He took a sip of coffee and began comparing the two files.

*CIA Trait: Anger/Perceived Insults/Injury.

*Org Study - Bayard: Prior to his assignment to the DAO office in Beirut, he was passed over for promotion from his rank as an E-6 Technical Sergeant to that of an E-8 Master Sergeant. He made no secret of the fact that, given his degree in International Affairs and his mastery of the Arabic language, he felt that he had been slighted in favor of other, clearly (to him), lesser deserving candidates.

*CIA Trait: Financial Need/Greed.

*Org Study - Bayard: Not very evident in his case. He seemed to have been living within his means throughout his Air Force career.

*CIA Trait: Adventurism/Thrill Seeking.

*Org Study - Bayard: The workup noted that he had volunteered for a military career. Upon listing in the Air Force, Bayard requested assignment for training in the elite Pararescue teams, or PJs. He failed to complete the selection process and was sent for electronics technical training. He later found a slot in the intelligence field and was granted a TS/SCI level clearance.

*CIA Trait: Ego/Self Image.

*Org Study - Bayard: As noted above, Bayard had a history of self-aggrandizement that was noted by more than a few of the sources in his background investigations.

*CIA Trait: Ingratiation/ Seeking Approval.

*Org Study - Bayard: See comments below.

*CIA Trait: Exploitive/Limited Sense of Guilt.

*Org Study - Bayard: Described by peers as initially having a friendly and charming personality. Other colleagues noted that their initial impressions of his behavior became less favorable, the longer they were exposed to him either socially or in the workplace.

*CIA Trait: A Pattern of Organizational Rule-Breaking.

*Org Study - Bayard: While this was not a pattern of his, Bayard had several minor security incidents which he initially attempted to blame on co-workers rather than himself.

*CIA Trait: Rationalization of the Crime.

*Org Study - Bayard: That remained to be seen.

= TWENTY-FIVE =

ABU SAIF

Ciudad del Este, Paraguay
September 29, 2004

Ciudad del Este is the second-largest city in the South American country of Paraguay. Located on the western side of the Parana River, it is one of the three cities, along with Puerto Iguazu of Argentina and Foz do Iguacu of Brazil, that comprise what is called the Tri-Border Area, or the TBA.

Ciudad del Este, the "City of the East" is a crowded municipality with a highly diversified population. Among the most common languages spoken in the area, in addition to the native Spanish, were Korean, Chinese, and Lebanese Arabic.

In 2004, the city was less than fifty years old, having been established in 1957. At its founding, the city was called Puerto Presidente Stroessner, in honor of its founder, the former military strongman General Alfredo Stroessner. Born of German parents and following a coup of his own design in 1954, Stroessner ruled the country for thirty-five years, or for eight consecutive terms as president.

Ciudad del Este was by no means a stranger to shady characters, whether those of the native variety or others of foreign extraction. Even less unusual were the shadier business dealings that the city and its inhabitants engaged in on a regular basis throughout its brief history.

The central business district was jammed to the gills with shops and traffic, both pedestrian and vehicular. Products of uncertain providence and legality were regularly on offer.

The congested streets of the city were overhung with questionably connected and tangled masses of electrical wiring. The discordant maze of smog, horns, voices and assorted noises comprised the ambiance of daily commerce.

Barely noticeable amidst the throng was a graying, middle-aged national from the northern Lebanese village of Batroun. Ghassan was slowly weaving his way into the central business district. It had been two hours since breakfasting at his home and it was time for business.

Ghassan had a specific financial transaction in mind for the day's activities - but it would not be a traditional wire transfer arrangement between established banks. He intended to use the traditional, more secure and time-honored system of the *hawala*.

The *hawala*, an Arabic word denoting the sense of trust, was a method of moving money over long distances via a covert network of proven intermediaries outside of the normal banking channels without leaving an electronic trace in their wake. It was operated by men called *hawaladars*, often as part of a more traditional front business, who knew that any cheating of customers would immediately ruin their business.

The system was as secure as it was simple. The customer approached a hawaladar in region and handed over the amount of cash that he wished to "send", along with a commission to cover the transaction. The hawaladar would then establish the account and give the customer a unique identity code for the transaction. Following that, he would contact a cooperating hawaladar at the other end of the transaction, advising the latter of the code and the amount to be paid out to the recipient.

When the intended recipient received the code from the sender, he passed this to the hawaladar on his end and was given the money. No identification or paper trail was needed. The two hawaladars would later settle their mutual accounts based on their own private arrangements.

Ghassan was on his way to see the man who was currently his favorite hawaladar - a man known to him as Abu Saif.

Midway down the crowded street, Ghassan found the shop he was looking for. A bit tattered and more than a bit time-worn, the shop was, somewhat unimaginatively called, *Cosas Electronicas.*

Stepping through the door, Ghassan caught sight of the owner's wife, Kalima. A plain, diminutive Lebanese woman, she wore a light blue hijab covering over her head and shoulders.

"Kalima," he greeted her. "*Kifek*?" How are you?

"I am well, Ghassan," she replied, recognizing him as a regular customer of the shop, though he did not usually appear as a purchaser of electronic devices.

"Would you like tea?" Kalima asked.

"Ah. Thank you. Very gracious of you. But no," he said. "Is Abu Saif here today?"

She nodded. "Yes. He is back in his office." She gestured toward a thin door in the rear. "Go on."

Kalima regarded the visitor with a calculated stare as he went to the back of the shop. She made it a practice to memorize all of the special customers. Such as this one.

A small bell jangled as Ghassan stepped into the back office. Abu Saif rose from his desk to greet him. "Ghassan," he said with a smile. "A long time. Good to see you again."

Abu Saif was a tall, light complected man with a full dark beard and flowing hair. Unlike many of the Lebanese in the city, he was wearing a flowing one-piece Islamic garb. He appeared to be in his mid-thirties and had a thickly built frame.

He was an immigrant to Paraguay. His name reflected his pride in the fact that he and Kalima had fathered a son that they named Saif, or "Sword." He was now Abu Saif - the father of Sword.

"*As-salamu alaikum*," Ghassan said, placing a hand on his heart.

"*Wa-alaikum salaam*," Abu Saif replied, returning to his chair. "How can I help you today?"

"Our usual business," Ghassan said, dropping his bulk into a padded seat. "I need to send some money to my cousin in Lebanon."

"Very well," Abu Saif said, reaching for a notebook on his desktop. "What are the details?"

"He is called Aadil," Ghassan said. "In the town of Byblos."

"Aadil...?"

"Aadil Harb," Ghassan completed.

"And the amount?" Abu Saif asked, jotting down the details.

"Fifteen thousand. American US dollars."

"Yes. And the password for this is?"

"Lazizah," Ghassan said. Or, delicious. "Hash tag 75."

Abu Saif nodded and recorded another half page of notes. "And the money, of course."

Without another word, Ghassan unzipped a fanny pack that was belted to his waist and withdrew a thick wad of US currency.

Carefully counting the bills out onto the desktop, he eventually displayed three hundred fifty-dollar notes.

"There. Fifteen thousand," he announced proudly. "Cash."

Abu Saif pulled the stack to himself and repeated the process. He counted though the bills until he saw the image of President Ulysses S. Grant pass through his fingertips another three hundred times. "Correct," he said at last.

"And your usual commission," Ghassan said, handing over another handful of bills.

Abu Saif accepted this with a curt nod and pushed them into a desk drawer.

"Anything else?" Ghassan asked.

"No, my friend," Abu Saif said, scratching out a receipt for his customer. "It will go through later today."

It was understood by both parties that a small commission would be subtracted on the Paraguayan and Lebanese sides of the transaction.

No physical money would actually move between the two countries. The transaction relied upon the levels of reputation and trust between the deposits and withdrawals of the two hawaladars on opposite side of the globe. Both receiving and disbursing sides would settle up with each other at a later date. It was the genius of the untraceable hawala system.

"*Ma'a salama,*" Ghassan said, rising to his feet.

"*Ma'a as-salama, Sadiqi,*" Abu Saif answered, shaking his hand and escorting him out of the shop.

Abu Saif paused at the entryway as he watched Ghassan push through the crowded sidewalk. Then, nodding to his wife, he returned to his office and closed the door.

Back at his desk, he jotted down a few more notes regarding the transaction, then dropped his notebook into the bottom desk drawer. As he closed the drawer, he caught sight of the familiar blue and white cloth rank insignia that protruded from the edge of the notebook.

It was the five inverted chevrons of a non-commissioned officer in the US Air Force - specifically that of an E-6 Technical Sergeant. They belonged to former Tech Sergeant, Intelligence NCO, and Arabic Linguist, Hank Bayard.

He locked the desk and slipped the key into his pocket.

That was another life. Another time.

= TWENTY-SIX =

INDUCTION

Bekaa Valley, Lebanon
1996-1997

In the waning days of October 1996, the staff members of the Defense Attaché's Office at the Beirut Embassy were planning an in-house Halloween party. However, amid the relatively cheery atmosphere, one of their NCOs, Air Force Technical Sergeant Henry Bayard, was planning something else entirely. To wit, desertion from his post and his subsequent defection from the United States.

Clearly, 1996 had been a busy one for the staff of the DAO, for many reasons, not the least of which had been dealing with the after-effects of the Israeli military operation called Grapes of Wrath.

Grapes of Wrath was an Israeli action conducted against southern Lebanon, primarily via air power. It was a response to Hezbollah rocket attacks on civilian settlements in northern Israel. As the Israelis readily admitted, the goal of the operation was to pressure the governments of both Lebanon and Syria to move forcefully against Hezbollah.

The operation began on April 11th with Israeli air and artillery strikes directed against Shia villages across the northern border. Along with the strikes were Israeli-broadcast messages urging the populace to leave the area. And so, they did. Hundreds of thousands of refugees abandoned their homes and fled northward toward Beirut.

Events progressed. By April 13th , the Israeli navy was successfully blocking the Lebanese ports of Beirut, Tyre, and Sidon. This was done to prevent the delivery of fresh weapons to Hezbollah. The world watched with mixed reactions.

And then, political disaster.

On April 18th, elements of Hezbollah established a mortar firing position adjacent to a UN refugee compound in the village of Qana. From there they lobbed mortar rounds upon an Israeli ground reconnaissance unit.

The Israeli Army replied with a fierce artillery shelling that killed over 100 refugees in Qana. A handful of UN soldiers from Fiji were also seriously wounded. This action resulted in widespread international condemnation of Israel and heavy diplomatic pressure to bring the operation to a close.

On the 25th , the United Nations Security Council passed Resolution 1052 which called for a cessation of hostilities on both sides. The short-circuited operation ended on the 27th of April, following an agreement brokered by France and the United States called the April Ceasefire Understanding. By that time, a reported 165 civilians had been killed and 401 more were wounded.

The Grapes of Wrath episode marked a breaking point for Hank Bayard. Since the beginning of his tour in Lebanon, he had been gradually and quietly becoming profoundly disaffected with US policy in the region. After reading after action reports of the operation, both open source and classified, he decided that he could not remain as part of what he saw to be the structure of oppression. The only question in his mind was when to make his move.

Originally, Bayard thought that he might slip away when his tour in Beirut was nearing its end. All of that changed, however, in mid-October when the DATT, an Army colonel, briefed the staff that a security team would be arriving from Germany within the next few weeks. As usual, the team would conduct refresher training, provide awareness briefings and conduct a limited number of vetting interviews with selected personnel.

It was the last bit, the vetting, that concerned Bayard. If he were to be one of the selected few, it could conceivably involve a session with a polygraph examiner.

While the polygraph had numerous critics, its results being inadmissible in court, adherents affirmed its value as an investigative tool at the very least. Indeed, its most useful application appeared to be the intimidation factor. It had the power to elicit pre-examination admissions from examinees for fear of otherwise being caught out by "the box."

While the holiday festivities were in full swing, Bayard slipped away from the Embassy compound and hiked several blocks to an awaiting car. There, a man that he had never met secured a woolen hood over his head, and he was driven to a safe house in a nondescript neighborhood of the capital. He was held there, locked in a single room, for the better part of two weeks while his Hezbollah handlers assessed the reaction to his disappearance.

When it was judged to be safe to move, Bayard was transported to an established training camp in a secluded area of the eastern Bekaa Valley.

Upon his arrival at the camp, Bayard was taken into custody by members of a section called *Amn al-Muddad*, Hezbollah's counterintelligence organization. Once again, he was locked into confinement, after which he was subjected to a lengthy and exhaustive series of interrogations to determine his bona fides.

They disdainfully referred to him simply as *Amrika*. America.

While a defector from the American Embassy was a welcome prospect, especially one with a Top Secret/SCI level clearance, the Muddad operatives were concerned that he may have been a plant, an attempt by Western Intelligence to infiltrate their ranks. It had happened before.

They need not have worried. It was while Bayard was an Arabic student at the Defense Language Institute in Monterey, California, that he had secretly converted to Islam. From his independent studies, he had become convinced of the justice of the Palestinian cause and, concomitantly, what he saw as the decades-long duplicitous policy of the US Government in the area.

Nevertheless, the Muddad questioning was hostile, bordering upon physical violence. At times, Bayard began to waiver in his commitment, wondering if his decision would result in his death. The threat of such a fate had certainly been presented more than once.

All of Bayard's carried personal belongings, admittedly not that much, had been taken away from him in the safe house. But it was not until he was in the hands of the Muddad men that the scrutiny of his possessions began in deadly earnest.

One object of particular interest that they found was a photograph of Vardah. It was something that he had been unable to part with.

Not being given to romanticism, the thoughts of his interrogators turned to darker things. What, for example, was this beautiful Lebanese woman doing with this rather average-looking American?

What, for example, if she was affiliated with the hated CIA? Or something even more sinister?

What if she was the mastermind behind an almost too-good-to-be-true plot to infiltrate the Party of God?

Discrete inquiries however, laid their concerns to rest. They found that she did have a reputation among a certain circle of people. And that reputation was disreputable. She was irreligious, a woman who readily associated with infidels. Worse, she made herself available to them for money. But she was, to all appearances, apolitical. Not a spy.

For his part, Bayard was questioned incessantly as to why he would be motivated to trade what they considered to be his privileged life as a Western infidel to join the jihad against his own people. As the sessions wore on, Bayard began to feel as though he were defending a thesis against a panel of harsh academic critics.

Eventually, the Muddad came to believe Bayard's story. His credibility was further boosted by a Lebanese national who worked for the DAO office. The Local gave a favorable review of Bayard's character, from the Hezbollah perspective, and supported his claim of a visiting security team that appeared after his disappearance.

Finally accepting the man *Amrika* as a true convert to both the religion and the cause, the Muddad surrendered him to the camp instructors. These consisted not only of Hezbollah veterans but also of advisors from the Iranian Quds Force.

The training consisted of the usual military topics of small unit tactics, map reading, explosives and ambushes. In Bayard's case, specialized training was provided in the practices of finance and the banking industry.

And they learned that he had yet another skill: Spanish language.

= TWENTY-SEVEN =

LIAISON REQUEST

Northern Virginia
October 4, 2004

Jake Kaczmar, the SAC of the DS Washington Field Office, was sitting at his desk idly staring through the windows of his office. The view across the parking lot revealed nothing more interesting than the sparse early morning traffic that was filtering along Gallows Road between Tyson's Corners to the north and Route 66 to the south. While mildly distracting, it was better than working on the soul-numbing statistics report that was soon due to Field Office Management in Rosslyn.

Refocusing, he abruptly picked up his phone and hit the button to call one of his Unit Supervisors.

"Sir?" a female voice replied, immediately recognizing the extension number of the caller.

"You have time to pop over here and see me now?" Kaczmar asked, not doubting the reply.

"Sure do," the supervisor replied. "Be there in a sec."

The individual he called was Leah's direct supervisor, Bobbie. As such, she had a key role in the joint DAY TRIPPER undercover case being run with the ATF agents in North Carolina. A DS traditionalist, going back to the old "SY", or Office of Security days, Kaczmar was still a bit leery of the undercover aspect, but he thought that something a bit more could still be done on it.

Within moments Leah's rail-thin Unit Supervisor appeared at the door, notepad and pen in hand. "What's up, Boss?" she asked.

"They tell me that you know the RSO down in Paraguay," he said, skipping the preliminaries.

"Sure do," she said. "That's Quig. Brian Quigley. I was on the Secretary's Detail with him a few years ago."

"What's his deal?"

"Ex-Border Patrol Agent. Did a first overseas tour in Lima. Married to a Peruvian, I think," she said, recalling the corridor gossip. "He was in Baghdad just before Asuncion. Good guy. Solid performer."

"If only such were true of all of them," Kaczmar muttered. He was thinking of two or three of his WFO agents who were now on the beach and being internally investigated for a variety of needless asininities.

"What's that again?"

"Nothing," he waved a hand dismissively. "I was just thinking about Leah's case with the ATF."

Bobbie nodded. Needless to say, she was all over it. The case had a lot of attention, ranging from the DS Headquarters in Rosslyn to the US Attorney's Office in Alexandria. And even now, the FBI was nibbling at the edges.

"Specifically," Kaczmar continued, "this Bayard guy. The one using the Adkins identity."

"Yep," she said. "Beirut DAO. The Air Force deserter."

"Correct. I think there's more to unearth about that character," Kaczmar said. "I'd like you to hit up CIL and have them send an expedited request for assistance out to your pal Quigley. Get him to see what the local cops down there can do to uncover anything about Bayard's location and activities. If possible... If he's even still there."

CIL was the Headquarters unit called Criminal Investigations Liaison. They handled the requests for international law enforcement cooperation between domestic DS entities and the various foreign police services.

"You got it," she said, taking a few notes on her pad. "It'll go it out this morning." She glanced up, "Anything else?"

"Yeah. And run it past your ASAC, of course, for his info," Kaczmar added needlessly, referring to her immediate superior, one of the Assistant Special Agents in Charge of the office.

"Right. Got it."

"Okay," Kaczmar said. He swiveled about in his chair to face his computer screen and returned to his updated stats report.

* * *

The next morning the DS Regional Security Officer for Paraguay, Brian Quigley, dropped into the chair behind his desk at Embassy Asuncion. He delicately placed the container of hot coffee from the cafeteria on the desktop and began to fire up his computer.

As the hard drive whirled to life, he turned his thoughts to his family's upcoming camping trip. Quigley was an outdoorsy type. Given the reversal of the seasons in the southern hemisphere, he was looking forward to making the most of the approaching summer months in Paraguay.

The screen came into view with agonizing slowness while he was focused on the upcoming excursion. After punching in his username and password, he waited once more as the overnight e-mails began to filter in, ever so slowly.

The one e-mail that immediately caught his eye was the high-priority message from DS/CIL. That particular office was not a usual communicant with his post.

Opening the message, Quigley saw that it was an RFOA, or official Request For Assistance, from CIL. They wanted him to contact his liaison in the local police with regard to a certain Henry Alan Bayard, also known as Thomas William Adkins. US Citizen. Fugitive. Believed to be now resident in Paraguay. A short bio of the man in question followed below the header.

Quigley was inspired by the news.

As was the case with all RSO's, given their extensive portfolio of responsibilities, including physical security, procedural security, counterintelligence, background investigations, VIP protection and the rest, each had their preferences. His heart was in the field of criminal investigations.

It grew from his days of what was called "cutting sign" or tracking and arresting interlopers along the southwest border as a US Border Patrol Agent. It expanded with his exposure to felony cases of passport and visa fraud later in his career as a DS Special Agent.

Bayard or Adkins, whoever the hell he was, Quigley knew that the best man to handle the RFOA was his primary liaison in the PNP. He reached for the phone and started the process.

* * *

The following afternoon Quigley visited his local contact, a certain Coronel Olivera, at the latter's office in the headquarters of the PNP, the *Policia Nacional del Paraguay*. As the name indicated, the PNP was the country's national law enforcement agency. It was subordinated to the Ministry of the Interior.

Olivera was the quintessential Latin version of a hail-fellow, well-met. He ran the unit that maintained contact with the security officers of the foreign diplomatic missions in the capital. He was especially close to the Americans.

Quigley came to the meeting with a gift in hand, as well as a request for a favor. Along with the RFOA from Washington, he brought along a bottle of the Coronel's favorite libation - Jameson Irish whiskey. Olivera happily accepted the gift. He promised to bring it along to an upcoming dinner that he would be hosting for his foreign colleagues, Quigley included.

As he had done before, Quigley dipped into his office's representational funds to purchase the whiskey from the embassy's own stocks. The use of representational funds was an authorized expense designed to schmooze with the locals or otherwise grease the skids of diplomatic maneuvering.

* * *

The Jameson proved to be a worthwhile investment. Within the week, *el Coronel* was back to Quigley with the information that his team had unearthed on the suspected American fugitive. Having been cautioned that this was still in the intelligence gathering stage, the PNP investigators limited themselves to running records checks and a brief spate of physical surveillance.

Unfortunately, the computer searches for a Norteamericano named Henry Bayard, or any H. Bayard, came up with zero results. There was no record of any such person ever being on the territory of the Republic of Paraguay, as a resident or otherwise.

The search for Adkins was a different story.

"We did, however, locate records of a US citizen named Thomas William Adkins," Olivera said. "He, or someone using that name, first entered the country though Immigration at our *Pettirossi Aeropuerto* three years ago. Whether he had already been here under another identity is matter of speculation."

"He came in on a US passport?" Quigley asked.

"Yes. An American blue tourist passport. Issued," he glanced down at his notes, "at your American consulate in Munich, Germany. In 2001."

"But probably our man Bayard, all the same," Quigley surmised.

"Quite possibly," Olivera agreed. "He entered and exited our country five times through Pettirossi since 2001. Routine photographs taken by our *Migracion* appear to match the one that you gave us."

"The one taken in North Carolina?"

"*Si*. The same."

Olivera referenced another set of files in his possession. "It appears however, that our *Senor* Adkins may be now living in the city of Ciudad del Este. According to our information, he may be operating an electronics shop under the name of *Anas Al Kitaab."*

"Al Kitaab," Quigley repeated. "Arabic for 'of the Book', unless I miss my meaning."

"Quite right," Olivera said. "And, also going by the name of Abu Saif."

"Gracias, Coronel," Quigley said, scooping up the PNP information. "Great work, as always. How can we thank you?"

"Well," Olivera began, "as you ask."

He went on to modestly explain that his eldest daughter, now a senior in high school with magnificent grades, had her heart set on attending the University of Miami in the *Estados Unidos*. Was there any possible way, he wondered, that Quigley could assist in this desire?

Quigley nodded. "*Por cierto*. Let me have her details and I'll see what can be done."

What he would do was to submit a routine referral request to the Consul General to obtain a student visa for Olivera's daughter. While Quigley was confident that she could probably qualify for the visa on her own, his intercession would form yet another bit of diplomatic adhesion between the already friendly parties.

"*Muchas gracias*, Senor Brian," Olivera said happily. "You will have the details tomorrow.

Quigley ended the day back at the embassy by banging out a cable to CIL in Rosslyn, passing along the new information.

Further action pending. He hoped.

= TWENTY-EIGHT =

YAQUB

Al Mazzeh District
Damascus, Syria
October 15, 2004

Astoundingly enough, from Yaqub Ghaziri's perspective, it had only been a few short weeks since his captivity by the Israelis. Not that he was by any means ungrateful for his rescue from the Jews by the Brothers. And now a rested and recovered Yaqub found himself in an office in the western environs of Damascus meeting with a senior Hezbollah official.

The office was now closed to visitors. The sun had long since dipped below the slopes of the historical Mount Qasioun. Otherwise known as Jabal Qasiyun, the mountain that was believed by some to be the home of the biblical Adam rose between the city of Damascus and his home in the Bekaa Valley.

His interlocutor, Ridwan by name, had long been known to Yaqub as a Hezbollah logistical facilitator. Friends, they were not. Professional associates – yes.

Ridwan was a Syrian national and a dentist by profession. While orthodontics provided the bulk of his above-board income, his deeper interests lie in the cause of political activism. Primarily, he was involved in the transportation of weapons and other militarily useful equipment from the Iranian suppliers in the east to the end users in Lebanon in the west.

Hezbollah, or the Party of God, was founded in Beirut in 1982. Right from its inception, Hezbollah was an instrument of Iranian foreign policy. The basis for its formation was its potential use as an Iranian proxy instrument in their struggle against Israel.

Insiders believe that Iran has been funding Hezbollah to the tune of $100 million per year. Others, equally well informed, suspect that the number is closer to $200 million. Such support appeared not only via cash shipments, but in terms of weaponry, training, and private charities and propaganda operations.

In the United States, while the 9/11 Commission found no connection between Hezbollah and the attacks, they did find that Iran and Hezbollah had allowed Al-Qaeda operatives to travel to both Iran (without stamping their Saudi passports as evidence of their visit) and the Bekaa Valley for training as early as 1992 and 1993.

Soon enough Hezbollah saw action as a participant in the 1992-1995 Bosnian civil war. There they sided with the Bosnian Muslims in that multi-sided conflict between the Muslims, the Bosnian Serbs, the national Serbs, and the Croats.

The decade of the nineties also saw Hezbollah's hand in bombings even further abroad. They were active against official Israeli and other Jewish targets in Buenos Aires, as well as the attack on the US Air Force facility in Khobar Towers in Saudi Arabia.

A major point of pride in their history was the guerrilla campaign in southern Lebanon which, in May of 2000, had resulted in the Israeli military withdrawal from the country.

Despite his trusted association with Yaqub, Ridwan was uncertain as to his most recent backstory. Clearly, by all accounts, the fellow had been an abductee of the Americans and a prisoner of the Israelis. His release was yet another story.

There were a number of Islamic factions operating in the south that had taken credit for his heroic rescue from the Israeli oppressors. Such a success would be yet another highly sought-after demonstration of bravado and machismo.

Who was the more believable as to his release? Ridwan had no idea. All that mattered was that Yaqub was now a free man and back in friendly hands. With a story to tell.

To enhance the aura of congeniality, a pot of hot, sweetened tea was served along with a plate of cookies and mints. Ridwan poured tea into a pair of dainty cups and sat back in his chair. "Thanks to God for your release from the hands of the Zionists," he began.

"Yes," Yaqub agreed, reaching for his teacup. "Allah be praised."

"You know," Ridwan continued, "when we heard that you were kidnapped from your home in Nahle, we all sadly assumed that you would soon be dead. Or locked away in Guantanamo."

"There is a difference?" Yaqub quipped weakly.

"So, it seems... Thankfully, God has returned you to your family."

"Yes."

"And now you come to us with some new information. Thanks to the stupidity of the Israelis."

"Yes."

"I have been told that you have become aware of a serious matter," Ridwan said. "In your own words, what is the issue of concern?"

Yaqub munched thoughtfully on a sugared cookie and followed it with another sip of tea. "I have never been one to spread stories or calumnies soiling the reputations of others."

"Of course not," Ridwan said, absently waving a hand. "Speak freely. As friend to friend."

"As I have written," Yaqub said, pushing a sealed envelope across the tabletop. "The Zionists. While they held me, it was their direct questions to me as well, as their comments that they assumed I could not hear. Or maybe they thought that I was too much of a peasant to comprehend."

"You understand the Hebrew language?"

"Some. Enough."

"Their mistake," Ridwan observed with a smile. "Go on."

"The issue was not with me," Yaqub said. "But with someone in Tehran, they said."

"Tehran?" Ridwan repeated. "How so?"

"They knew that I was involved in financial support of our fighters. But they seemed to think that I knew about foreign funding going to a high level source in Iran. In the capital. Tehran."

"What sort of foreign funding?"

"They didn't say. I assumed American. Or Israeli."

"So why ask you about this matter?"

Yaqub shrugged. "They did not ask directly. They implied that they had a source in our organization."

"In our organization, you say?" Ridwan repeated, eyebrows furrowing.

Yaqub nodded. "In the organization of our benefactors, more likely. In the organization of Iran. I presumed."

Calmly and gently, Ridwan led his guest though another thirty minutes of questioning. The Lebanese man recounted his capture by the Americans, the intense questioning by the Israelis and finally the dramatic release into the arms of his daring comrades.

The key elements of his information gathered, Ridwan generously expended another half hour of his evening, recounting their shared experiences and sacrifices in the struggle against the Zionists. At last, he glanced at his wristwatch and declared the meeting to have come to an end.

Thanking him once again for his suffering, Ridwan took possession of the envelope on the tabletop containing Yaqub's written report. In return, he slid another envelope across in Yaqub's direction. It contained a small packet of Lebanese pound notes as recompense for his troubles.

Yaqub bobbed his head and touched his heart in appreciation of the gesture. He then bade farewell and rose to leave.

Ridwan had already concluded that an urgent meeting with his Iranian handler was in order. The handler would want to get this information back to Tehran as soon as possible.

As he watched his old friend depart, Ridwan silently acknowledged that, while his associate had provided a valuable service, he nevertheless now held a dangerous secret in his head. Ridwan made a mental note that Yaqub Ghaziri deserved close observation from now on. And, if necessary, removal.

If needed, the removal would be done in a manner that was more efficient than either the Americans or the Israelis had proved capable of.

= TWENTY-NINE =

RUDAKI'S SHADOW

Rudaki Park
Dushanbe, Tajikistan
October 20, 2004

The Bosniak who called himself Escobar was a long-time JICSA asset. Prior to his association with the Org, he had developed a reputation for his youthful, if unpalatable, association with the Sarajevo underworld. Although initially frowned upon by the community, his proclivity toward violence gained greater acceptability as the Bosnian conflict of the 1990's split the agonized society into numerous warring factions.

Given his colorful background, which by then was a marketable commodity, he was often called upon for his strong-arm skills. In the fullness of time, the Org took notice.

At the moment, Escobar was lounging across the street from the Hotel Avesto. The hotel was in central Dushanbe, the capital of Tajikistan, just east of the Varzob River. It was still mid-morning and the weather, given the time of year, was chilly but more than agreeable.

Escobar zipped up his jacket a notch and resisted the urge to look at his watch. There was no need for it, as he was well aware of the impending time crunch.

The Avesto was an oddly constructed structure. One of Dushanbe's many Soviet-era hotels, its five-story gray and green façade was a testament to what had, at least, been an effort to create something that was a bit new and different.

Accustomed as he was to the many bullet-pocked facades of the socialist-inspired buildings of his native Sarajevo, the Avesto looked pretty good to him.

And then at last, his target finally appeared.

The man that Escobar was expecting emerged onto the sidewalk in front of the Avesto and paused to survey the surroundings. He was an unimposing figure; middle-aged, with glasses, bearded and balding.

Escobar had no need to refer to the photo that was secreted in his jacket pocket. He had studied the image of Shahriar Parviz many more times than enough before posting himself outside of the Avesto. There was no doubt that figure across the street from him was the focus of his surveillance.

Parviz was right on schedule. Apparently confident that he was free of any possible Iranian surveillance, he headed out toward the scheduled clandestine meeting with the individual that he assumed to be his French case officer.

As the Org knew, Parviz was in Dushanbe on an officially sanctioned mission for the MOIS. His approved assignment was the routine inspection of the MOIS station in the Iranian Embassy, with a special focus on their on-going coverage of the US Embassy and its staff. As such, the trip afforded him a relatively risk-free opportunity to meet with the man he knew as Alban.

* * *

Hawk was already waiting for Parviz in Rudaki Park, the main city green of Dushanbe. He was sitting on a wooden bench, cradling a plastic bottle of cold tea in his hands. Not far away, across the sprinkling fountain of waters, was the statue of Abu Abdallah Jafar ibn Mohammad al-Rudaki. The statue stood under a faded blue arch that was replete with images of stars and sunbursts.

Born in the ninth century AD, Rudaki, the so-called "Adam of Poets," was considered to be the father of Persian poetry. Unfortunately, after serving as the court poet to the Islamic Samanid rulers, he lost the favor of the court and eventually died in abject poverty.

Nevertheless, after the fall of the Soviet Union, the new Tajik Republic needed national heroes of its own, along with a fresh sense of history. Rudaki was selected for a leading role in that pursuit.

As Hawk waited, a text message popped into his phone. It was from Zlatko, who was posted at the entrance of the park. The text announced that Parviz had entered the park and for all intents appeared to be free of hostile surveillance.

He acknowledged the message to the effect that all was good on his side as well.

Within minutes the figure of the Iranian officer came into view. He approached confidently and, for all appearances, randomly dropped into place at the other end of the bench without exchanging glances with Hawk.

"*Monsieur* Alban," he said quietly, his eyes focused elsewhere. "Good to see you once again."

"And you as well," Hawk replied, still gazing straight ahead.

"I do not have much time today," Parviz said. "Business awaits. What news do you have for me?"

"There is news," Hawk said. "It may pertain to your friend back home," he added, referring to Mokri. "Possibly as a means of attacking him."

Parviz pulled a copy of the local newspaper, the *Farazo*, out of his jacket pocket and unfolded it. "You have my attention," he said, his face impassive.

"Do you still have contacts in Lebanon? The Bekaa Valley?"

"Of course."

Hawk nodded. "Is the name Yaqub Ghaziri familiar to you?"

Parviz pursed his lips momentarily as he ostensibly studied the newspaper. "No," he admitted. "Not that I can recall."

Hawk took a sip of his tea. "It might be profitable to look into him," he said. "He appears to be a financier of your friends in the Bekaa." Neither wished to voice the word *Hezbollah.*

"Most interestingly," Hawk continued, "this fellow Ghazi recently escaped from Israeli custody after being forcibly taken from his village."

"Taken? Taken by whom?"

Hawk shrugged. "Presumably either by the Israelis or the Americans... We do not know for sure."

"Israelis, most likely," Parviz said. "The Americans are too gun-shy for such matters. They have far too much going on in the Mid-East as it is already."

"A reasonable assessment," Hawk agreed.

The men fell silent as a group of Asian tourists ambled by the bench, gawking and pointing at the Rudaki statue.

"How is this Yaqub useful to our enterprise?" Parviz prompted, once they had passed.

"It might seem that not all of the Israelis are as security conscious as they appear," Hawk allowed. "According to this Yaqub fellow, he overheard comments about a possible high-level Israeli source in Tehran."

Parviz frowned. "And this is verified by your official contacts?"

"Of course."

Parviz could not help glancing over at the man he thought to be his French case officer. "And you think that this source is Javed Mokri?" he asked.

Hawk frowned. "Whatever the truth of the matter, it could be made to appear that he is the Jewish source. This would help your case, would it not?"

"It would be useful," Parviz agreed, pointedly looking at his watch.

"Even more so if you could provide his supervisors with hard evidence of his treachery," Hawk said, floating the idea.

Parviz risked a quick glance in "Alban's" direction. "How would this be possible?"

Hawk wagged his head noncommittally. "Maybe something to discuss in the future."

Sensing that the meet was coming to an end, Hawk pushed a bit further. "And do you have anything for me today?"

The Iranian nodded almost imperceptibly. "We have identified two officers of interest at the American Embassy here," he said. "One is a political officer; the other is a communicator. The first is having an extramarital affair. The other seems to have more than a passing interest in the local drug culture."

Parviz dropped the newspaper onto the bench between them. "The names are there," he said.

"Good to know," Hawk agreed, casually gathering up the paper.

Parviz straightened his jacket and clambered back to his feet. "*A bientot,*" he said, departing.

= THIRTY =

TASK FORCE ORANGE

Airborne Out of Dushanbe
October 28, 2004

The day after his meeting with Parviz, Hawk was on a commercial flight back to the States and reflecting on the next steps of the case. After the plane reached its cruising altitude, he ordered a gin and tonic and unfolded an English language newspaper. One of the articles covered what was being called The Battle of Samarra.

Several days earlier, it read, some 3,000 US troops, accompanied by 2,000 Iraqi soldiers, had entered Samarra. The area was a city on the Tigress River, north of Baghdad. Their mission was to drive the insurgents, who had already seized Fallujah and Ramadi, out of the city. According to the news report, they were successful in doing as after heavy house-to-house fighting.

Hawk had the dubious pleasure of visiting Iraq a number of times during his Army career. The date of his last visit was two years earlier.

Baghdad, Iraq
Summer 2002

The year was 2002 and Saddam Hussein was in power. Several months earlier, President George Bush had designated Iraq as part of what he called the Axis of Evil. The other members of the Axis were Iran and North Korea. All were so designated for their suspected involvement in weapons of mass destruction (WMD) and proven record of human rights violations and enmity to the United States and the West in general.

By July Saddam had further enhanced his international reputation as a malevolent figure by once again ejecting a team of United Nations weapons inspectors from an agreed-upon visit to Iraq.

Hawk's ISA unit was then operating in Iraq under the then-current nom de guerre of Task Force Orange. It was to be Hawk's final overseas deployment prior to his retirement from the Army. And it was to be a good one.

Their target, however, was not Saddam himself, but one of his in-country guests. The prey was a noted terrorist who called himself Abu Nidal - or the Father of Struggle.

The man's true name was Sabri Khalil al-Banna. He was a 65-year-old Palestinian who had been born into a well-to-do family in the Mediterranean coastal town of Jaffa. At the time of his birth, in 1937, Jaffa was part of the British Mandate. After 1948, Jaffa became part of Israel, and al-Banna became a refugee.

At the beginning of his terrorist career the displaced Palestinian allied himself with none other than Yasser Arafat, chairman of the Palestine Liberation Organization (PLO). This association lasted until 1974 when it collapsed. The breakup was fueled by a basic disagreement over operational strategy. Arafat favored concentrating the PLO attacks exclusively on Israeli targets. Al-Banna, on the other hand disagreed, insisting on pursuing the wider range of international targets.

Falling away, al-Banna established his own crew of extremists. It was called the Abu Nidal Organization (ANO), also known as the Fatah Revolutionary Council.

As Hawk admitted to his colleagues, whatever al-Banna's faults, he could not be faulted for his lack of committed follow-through. Between the years of 1974 and 1992, his

ANO was credited with more than 90 terrorist attacks in 20 different countries. His victims, either killed or wounded, exceeded 900 people. He was also sentenced to death in absentia not only by a Jordanian military court, but for attacks on his fellow Palestinians as well.

Unsurprisingly, al-Banna's actions also drew the attention of the US Government. Among his critics was the US State Department, which called the ANO "the most dangerous terrorist organization in existence." In the National Security Council, the soon-to-be-famous Lieutenant Colonel Oliver North declared him to be "public enemy number one."

Clearly, it was determined in the upper reaches of the counter-terrorism elite in Washington, something had to be done. That decision involved covert military action.

Hawk's ISA team had been infiltrated into a hostile Iraq with the mission of locating al-Banna. Although the intelligence community, primarily the Defense Intelligence Agency (DIA), had a good idea of his location, that considered estimate had to be confirmed. And once that was confirmed, he needed to be tracked so that his probable locations could be determined. After his habits and daily routines, otherwise known as his pattern of life, were ascertained with a high level of confidence, it would be time to call in members of yet another so-called Tier One unit.

And they would end him.

Once the team settled into their Baghdad safe house, the techie knob turners began their electronic sweeps, methodically scrubbing the electronic spectrum in search of al-Banna's phones and other devices. Hawk and his HUMINT partners, on the other hand, began probing the area for likely human source candidates. Along with the team was a female soldier named Yara. She was an Arabic linguist who had been born in Jordan. She would be invaluable when it came to communicating with the locals in their own language, free of nuance.

And thanks to the DIA leads, they were able to develop three of them. all were carefully interrogated by Hawk, with the assistance of Yara. Of the trio, the more promising one was a man named Benji who was employed as in a relatively unglamorous position as a char force supervisor. But the duties of his position were not important; the location was. The source worked in a building where al-Banna was thought to be living.

By mid-August, the team believed that they had him. Surveillants were confident that they had "eyes on" and had identified the vehicles that he appeared to be using. On Saturday the 17th, the team sent out the message that the target location was confirmed and that the awaiting Tier One operators could enter the area to execute the mission. On the following day, the off-site commander confirmed that the so-called action guys were preparing to go inbound to Baghdad.

Then, on Monday the 19th, Benji called in with an emergency message. Something of significance had happened, but exactly what had happened was not clear. Hawk summoned the ISA source for a hurried meeting with himself and two other ISA operatives - including Yara.

Later that evening a shaken Benji appeared at a safe house to meet with Hawk, Yara, and an armed backup. After few calming cups of tea, Benji explained that something had happened at the apartment of al-Banna that morning. As Yara corrected his convoluted English, Benji reported that a number of aggressive men came to the building unbidden. Although they were dressed in civilian clothes, they were, he said, clearly from the *Mukhabarat*, or the security service.

There was an audible scuffle in the apartment, Benji said. Followed by gunfire.

Shortly thereafter, another team of men arrived in an ambulance. They clambered up to the apartment and soon left, lugging what appeared to be a human figure encased in a zippered-up, black plastic body bag.

Another spending another twenty minutes probing further for more details, but failing in the effort, they ended the debrief. Yara handed Benji an envelope full of Iraqi dinars and sent him on his way. After Benji departed, Hawk scrambled to call off the entry of the hit team, at least until the situation could be better understood.

Answers came quickly.

The very next day, the word came out that Sabri Khalil al-Banna had been found dead in his apartment. According to the Iraqi authorities, he had committed suicide while being interrogated by the police. Supposedly, al-Banna had broken away from his interrogators and fled into his bedroom where he shot himself to death.

Palestinian sources would counter this with the assertion that he had been shot not once but numerous times. According to this version of events, Saddam had ordered the execution for fear what al-Banna might do in the event of a possible American invasion.

Regardless of the true perpetrator, Hawk's team was ordered out of the area. Their mission - by whatever means - had been accomplished.

= THIRTY-ONE =

RIDWAN

Al Mazzeh District
Damascus, Syria
November 15, 2004

Doctor Ridwan was staying late in his dental offices that evening to review incoming paperwork, admittedly little of which had to do with the field of dentistry. The majority of the documents were, in fact, related to the financial affairs of his activist brothers in Hezbollah.

The people in Tehran were expressing mild concern, bordering on amusement, with regard to a recent United Nations Security Council Resolution. Passed two months earlier, Resolution 1559 had called for the disarmament of all militia groups in Lebanon. For their part, the leaders of Hezbollah declined the offer. In doing so, they justified their retention of weapons by asserting that they were the sole defenders of Lebanon against Israeli aggression and therefore could not, and would not, disarm.

Ridwan whispered a mild expletive to the empty room, describing his views of the United Nations and the worth of its various resolutions.

Another report cited ideas for expanding the financial scope of Hezbollah operations. Contacts in Asia and Latin America were of special interest to the analysts.

One document of particular concern related to the Yaqub man, Yaqub Ghaziri by name. Yaqub of Nahle. Or, more precisely, the former Yaqub of Nahle.

He was dead.

Ridwan took no pleasure in the news. Nor was it unexpected, as he himself had made the arrangements. Now, although a good man was gone from this earth, so was his tale of a possible Israeli agent in Tehran. He had purchased time to study the problem. To work the problem, as the Americans might say.

But returning his attention to the present. He had been made aware of the fact that a promising source of funding was being handled by a hawaladar in Paraguay. And not only was this brother a reliable channel of continuing funds, but he was also an American. And more than that, he was a believer who had turned his back on the Great Satan.

And that, he thought, could be a useful bit of information.

= THIRTY-TWO =

CAYMAN

George Town, The Cayman Islands
November 17, 2004

The Cayman Islands are an autonomous overseas territory of the United Kingdom, with a royal history dating back to 1670. They are separated from Miami via a commercial flight of little more than an hour. Basking in the Caribbean sun south of Cuba, the islands enjoy the bulk of their business trade from the tourism industry.

Tourists are not the only people who are attracted to the lure of the islands, however. According to the US State Department, the Caymans are cited as a jurisdiction of primary concern for offshore money laundering and associated financial crimes.

Despite their modest size, that being only one and a half times as large as the area of Washington, DC, the Caymans are listed among the top banking centers on Earth. They rightly claim trillions of dollars in assets that are distributed among more than 150 banks. Boasting some of the most stringent banking secrecy laws on the international scene, the Caymans also host the majority of the world's hedge funds.

Hedge funds, along with private equity firms, are recognized as entities that are highly vulnerable to criminal manipulation. That is because vast amounts of money comes and goes through their channels with few questions asked as to their source or destination. According to one informed estimate, the total number of hedge funds surged by three hundred percent after 2001.

One of the many secretive financial institutions located in the capital city of George Town on Grand Cayman was the suitably named Britannicus Holdings, Limited. Britannicus was an aggressive player in hedge funds and similar such financial enterprises.

One of the mid-level officers of Britannicus was a diminutive, fortyish man of foreign origin. A single and solitary figure, his associates commonly referred to him as The Armenian.

In truth, he was an actual Armenian. Back in the day, and certainly unknown to his colleagues, he had been a junior officer of the KGB of the Armenian Soviet Socialist Republic – the agency that was now called the National Security Service.

His specialty in the Armenian KGB had been covert finance and logistics in support of operations. Although once seen as a promising up-and-comer, his luster slowly faded along with his failing marriage to the daughter of a senior politico. And with it, his career prospects faded just as quickly.

As promotions slowed and professional expectations dimmed, he became more focused on the advantages presented by his actual duties. Inevitably, the more he was exposed to the ease of the financial flows and the varied expenditures, the more he was tempted to divert some of the money for himself.

To his pleasant surprise, diverting money from the official accounts, in small amounts and then in ever larger increments, was not all that difficult. At least, not for someone with the required expertise. And with that came a marginally better life. And the women. And cocaine.

He was past the cocaine bit now. For the most part.

Nevertheless, embezzling from the coffers of the KGB entailed an insanely high element of risk. That was true whether it involved pilfering from the Armenian KGB or from their big brothers in Moscow. He eventually came to realize that a dangerous threshold had been irrevocably crossed.

Somehow, news of his plight reached the ears of the Americans. How that happened, he never knew and was never told.

In any event, one evening while drinking alone at a Yerevan nightclub, a local national cautiously approached him with a tentative offer of help. Although apprehensive and professionally suspicious, he expressed a degree of interest. The local national subsequently put him in touch with an elderly gentleman who appeared to have solid contacts with a US government agency headquartered in Langley, Virginia.

The Virginian proved to be a source of possible salvation. Apparently well informed, he fully comprehended the Armenian's situation and offered him a legitimate way out, to include covering some of his past financial sins. However, the deal involved The Armenian's agreement to remain in place for a bit longer, followed by an escape mechanism and a secure life in another country.

Before very much longer, The Armenian was an active and valued agent in place in the service of American Intelligence.

For several years, The Armenian functioned as a productive American agent. His contributions included biographical assessments of senior Armenian KGB officers, reports of ongoing operations against the West and penetration attempts of the US Embassy staff via the local employees, also known as Foreign Service Nationals, or FSNs.

However, despite the best of intentions, nothing lasts forever. Slightly more than a year before the 1991 independence of Armenia, he found his situation in the KGB to be untenable. As promised, the Americans had an escape route prepared for him as well as a follow-up life under a protected identity abroad.

Where that follow-up life eventually took him to was George Town, Cayman Islands, with a comfortable position in the financial sector. It included the explicit understanding that he would be available to assist Langley on an as-needed basis. Now was one of those times.

The Armenian had been involved in this particular caper for the past two months. From his original contact in Miami, he was aware that the target was an Iranian named Javed Mokri. He knew little of Iranian issues and had even less interest in the topic.

Nevertheless, following his instructions, The Armenian began to build a money trail for the mysterious Mr. Mokri. Using a substantial, yet temporary, cash flow out of Miami, he set up a trail showing an inflow of deposits into Britannicus from an obscure hawaladar in Paraguay and several other foreign sources.

Thanks to his machinations, some of the money appeared to have been invested in a cruise ship line and other businesses with the proceeds moving out of the Caribbean to another bank in Geneva, Switzerland.

In the event, the true Javed Mokri actually did have an account in the targeted Swiss bank. It was under an assumed name that, while unknown to The Armenian, was indeed known to the Iranian MOIS.

Crucially, one of the entities ostensibly sending money into the Swiss Mokri account could be traced to a bona fide Israeli source that was housed in a bank in Berlin. This was unlikely to be well received, once uncovered by the MOIS and higher authorities in Tehran.

After recounting his actions in painstaking detail, The Armenian glanced up at the olive-skinned man with the American accent who was sitting on the other side of his desk. "The evidence of money flows into this Swiss account has been established. This is what we have agreed to. Yes?" he asked.

"Correct," Chalice said. He crossed his legs, wincing a bit as a small flash of pain shot through his gut. It was his first overseas deployment after his discharge from the hospital. With JD Tucker's approval, he was slowly working his way back into operations.

And what better operation to engage in than the one crafted around his own revenge?

= THIRTY-THREE =

SHEBA'A FARMS

Southern Lebanon
December 15, 2004

Shahriar Parviz pulled the rough collar of his jacket up over his neck. While camouflage clothing was not his usual attire, today's apparel was obligatory. And it was fairly comfortable in the windy 60-degree temperatures.

Parviz slightly adjusted his position in an attempt to find a bit more comfort. Swearing softly under his breath, he found that his efforts were futile. The holstered pistol on his side was still irritatingly digging into his bones.

The MOIS officer was lying prone on the ground amid a clump of bushes. With one hand, he braced a pair of binoculars against his eyes. With the other, he adjusted their focus to get a better view of the landscape ahead. Glassing the target, as the military would say.

A few meters away from him, off to his right, were three locals. All were members of Lebanese Hezbollah. With them was a fellow Iranian named Arash . He was an officer of the IRGC, the Islamic Revolutionary Guard Corps.

With the assistance of their Iranian brethren, Hezbollah was developing a style of fighting in what was later to be termed as hybrid warfare. This method combined regular forces with guerrilla groups, as well as weaponizing social media for both information and disinformation efforts.

Yet, as Parviz well knew, today's operation would fall strictly withing the category of kinetic strikes.

The Hezbollah men were deftly loading a projectile into the tube of an RPG-7. The weapon was a Russian-made anti-tank rocket launcher. Its warhead was essentially a shaped charge, designed to explode only after punching through the skin of an armored vehicle.

They were in the area known as Sheba'a Farms. It was a strip of land located in Southern Lebanon, on the border with Syria and the Golan Heights. It was a contested area, claimed by all parties concerned. And occupied by Israel since 1967.

The ground that Parviz was studying was called *Har Dov*, or Mount Dov, by the Zionists. They named it after Dov Rodberg, an Israeli Army Captain who was killed there in 1970. He would soon have company.

Staring through the lenses of the binoculars, Parviz could clearly see a handful of green-uniformed men across the way. They were soldiers of the IDF, or Israeli Defense Forces. Next to them was an Army jeep and an American-made M113 armored personnel carrier. Both were stationary, for the moment.

The M113 was a tracked infantry vehicle that dated its provenance back to the days of the Vietnam War. The back ramp of the APC was down. Several soldiers had exited the track and were casually mulling about. Easy pickings.

Parviz had been ordered to attend this operation as an official observer on behalf of the MOIS. As was the case with the majority of his colleagues, he greatly resented the IRGC and their growing interference in intelligence and other covert activities. Although Parviz had no issues with killing Israelis, as such, he did not necessarily feel that such small-scale projects were in the best interests of the Republic.

Nevertheless, here he was with Arash. The latter was a prime example of IRGC arrogance: cocky, self-assured, and keen to attack.

After several more minutes of quiet preparation, Arash wagged his hand in Parviz's direction. Team ready. Parviz nodded in response.

Moments later, one of the Hezbollah fighters pulled the trigger on the shouldered RGP-7.

Instantly, the rocket exited the tube and flashed across the fields of Sheba'a Farms. Reaching its destination within seconds, it penetrated the aluminum alloy side armor of the M113 and detonated inside the boxy crew compartment.

The initial blast was quickly followed by a secondary explosion as the stored ammunition within blew. The soldiers outside of the M113 all dropped to the ground, either having been wounded by the attack, reacting in shock, or diving to take cover. Regardless, there was no return fire from the Israelis.

As they had been previously coached, the Hezbollah men did not advertise their position by any cheering or waving. Cautiously, they and their two Iranian advisors carefully backed out of their firing position and escaped to safety.

Parviz nevertheless made a mental note to advise his French intelligence contact, Monsieur Alban, of the incident.

= THIRTY-FOUR =

7 FAM

Dunn Loring, Virginia
December 21, 2004

Tuesday morning. Christmas was coming and the DS Washington Field Office was short staffed between vacations and assignments to a variety of protective details.

Leah and her unit supervisor, Bobbi, were waiting in the WFO conference room when SAC Kaczmar finally entered.

"Sorry for the delay," Kaczmar said, dropping a notebook and pen onto the tabletop and settling into a chair. "Was on the phone with the folks at Field Office Management. Budget stuff."

"No prob," Bobbi said.

"Okay Bobbi", Kaczmar began, flipping open the notebook. "Since your ASAC is on a SecState trip to Jordan right now, you have the ball. This thing with the guy in Paraguay. Still moving forward?"

"Right."

"And so then, are we good with the 7 FAM?" he asked.

The FAM, or the Foreign Affairs Manual, comprised a series of policy and operational guidance that governed the activities of the State Department. In this case, 7 FAM 1620 was appropriately titled Extradition of Fugitives to the United States.

"Leah and I were down at EDVA yesterday," Bobbi said, referring to the office of the federal prosecutors at the

Eastern District of Virginia in Alexandria. “One of the newer guys agreed to take this one up.”

“We confirmed that the US does have an active extradition treaty with Paraguay,” Leah chimed in. “It was negotiated under Clinton in November of 1998 and went into effect in March of 2002. Still good.”

Kaczmar uncapped his gel pen and poised it over a blank notebook page. "Who's the AUSA?" he asked, referring to the Assistant US Attorney assigned to the case.

"Sanon," Bobbi said. "Guillaume Sanon. Haitian."

"Spell that." Pen scratching.

She did.

"Guillaume any good?"

Bobbi shrugged. "Like I said, he's fairly new. But eager to start taking our cases."

"Then Guillaume's our guy," Kaczmar said, jotting another note.

"He has me booked in for the Grand Jury next week," Leah added "He'll get Bayard indicted on Passport Fraud and a few other charges. Then we'll ask a magistrate to issue a Provisional Arrest Warrant."

"He also mentioned charges of being a deserter from the Air Force," Bobbi said.

Kaczmar rolled his eyes upward in refection. "Um... I had a case a while back involving a military deserter. As I recall, the statute of limitations runs out on that charge after five years. And Bayard’s been gone, what, seven, eight years now?"

Bobbi shook her head. "Negative, Boss. Sanon said that the five years are suspended if the target is outside of US jurisdiction."

"And the NLETS travel data doesn’t show him coming back into the States after his disappearing act from Beirut," Leah added. "Either in his Bayard identity or the one he's using down there now."

"Okay then," Kaczmar said. "Update the RSO."

= THIRTY-FIVE =

THE TBA

US Embassy
Asuncion, Paraguay
January 11, 2005

Brian Quigley, the Regional Security Officer at Embassy Asuncion, readjusted himself in his chair as he regarded the young DS Special Agent on the other side of his desk.

Leah Chaikin had arrived in-country the previous afternoon. Having been met by an Embassy expediter, she was picked up and delivered to her hotel to spend the night. And here she was.

"Nice to finally meet you," Quigley said. "Your case has caused a bit of a stir down here. But a nice diversion, as far as I'm concerned."

"Good to be here," she said. "First time in South America."

"But same time zone," Quigley said. "So, no jet lag."

"There's that," she agreed.

"A newbie?" he asked, sliding a cup of chocolaty Paraguayan coffee in her direction. "Don't recognize your name."

"Yes," she said. "WFO is my first tour. I was a probation officer in Maryland prior to this. Bidding out this summer. Hopefully Dublin or Moscow."

"Hopefully," Quigley agreed. But maybe Iraq or West Africa, he was thinking.

"Okay, where are we?" he said, taking a sip of his coffee.

Answering his own question, he continued, "Post received the provisional arrest warrant. The LegAtt is looped in. My pal, Colonel Olivera, over at the PNP, is still good with it."

"Right."

"And you have a date with the Core Country Team members tomorrow morning to brief them up on the history of the case and answer any questions they might have. They're okay with it but would have rather not had the aggravation, to tell you the truth."

"Got it."

"But," he went on, "We also have a note from WFO to the effect that the timing of the arrest is still up in the air."

"Also correct."

"So, what's up with that? Exactly?"

"There's a, uh, another team coming to town. Also focused on Bayard. Not law enforcement though. Something else. Your *Other People* here will be in the know by now."

"More of that," Quigley said, rolling his eyes slightly. "And?"

"And the arrest will be good to go, as soon as they finish their op. Whatever it is."

= THIRTY-SIX =

THE WILD, WILD SOUTH

Ciudad Del Este, Paraguay
January 13, 2005

Bear and Hawk were perched in the rear of an ancient Toyota HiAce van. They were peering through the blackened windows at the shop that was across the street and a half block down. "*Cosas Electronicas*" read the sign above the door.

The shop had a shabby, down-on-its-luck, appearance. Not all that out of place however, situated as it was along a street that was overhung with a tangle of twisted power lines. Purloined electricity, Bear thought. A common enough thing, from all appearances.

It was mid-morning but already sweltering in the enclosed van. They had earlier caught sight of a man, who could well have been Hank Bayard, and a woman, who could have well been his wife, unlocking the front door and opening the shop.

"Sweating my butt off in mid-January," Bear complained, taking another swallow of tepid water from a plastic bottle. "More comfy back in Vietnam at this time of year."

"Reversed seasons," Hawk murmured, looking at a notebook. "Warmest month of the year around these parts."

"Great," Bear griped. "Makes me feel better already."

"This is interesting, “Hawk continued. "According to my notes, it looks like Bayard also filed for something called a CC5 account in Brazil awhile back."

"Which is what?"

Hawk frowned. "From what I see, the CC5 was something set up in the late '60s for non-resident companies and individuals. They also served to help foreign companies do foreign wire transfers to send money back home. Illegally."

"Clever guy," Bear observed.

"Yeah, well... I don’t think we're going to see much more here today," Hawk said, grunting as he climbed back into the driver’s seat of the Hice.

"In all my years of travel," Bear said, settling into the passenger’s seat, "I've never been down in these parts. You?"

"This is my first time in Paraguay," Hawk said. "But not in the region."

"Yeah?"

"Bolivia."

Bear took another swig of water. "Well, seeing as how we seem to have time on our hands, tell me a war story."

Hawk turned the ignition and reached for his own water bottle. "It was a little while back," he said. "After a DEA agent named Casimiro was kidnapped in the Chapare Province."

"Chapare?"

"Rural area of the Cochabamba Department in central Bolivia. It's about the size of New Jersey."

Bear shook his head. "Doesn’t help."

Hawk shrugged, "Chapare was a major coca-producing area. Cocaine. Still is as far as I know."

"Yeah?"

"Back in 1987," Hawk continued, "the DEA started an operation in Bolivia called Snowcap. As part of that effort, DEA funded an anti-narcotics group called the Rural Mobile Patrol Unit. Better known as the Leopards."

"And this Casimiro was with the Leopards," Bear conjectured, recalling his own history of working undercover with the DEA.

"Yes, as an advisor," Hawk said. "But the story was that Casimiro was with a patrol that was ambushed. Two or three of the Leopards were killed, and he was taken prisoner by the Cartels."

"Okay."

"But," Hawk said, "the DEA was still smarting, understandably, from the abduction, torture and murder of their agent Kiki Camarena. That was in Guadalajara, 1985. Mexico. They didn't want a repeat of that in Bolivia."

"You said, 'the story,'" Bear prompted. "That's the true story?"

Hawk maneuvered the van silently through traffic for a few seconds before speaking again. "In actuality, Casimiro was not kidnapped. Somewhere along the way, he apparently determined that the Narcos were able to pay him at a significantly higher level than his GS-whatever civil service salary. So, on that day, he walked the Leopards into an ambush that killed several and then he disappeared into the woods."

"And then?"

"And then came the Org," Hawk said. "I was on a team that was made up mostly of Salvadoran mercs. Tough little guys. We were sent into the Chapare to find Casimiro. And we did."

"And he's not coming back," Bear completed the thought for him. "Damn, I never heard that story before."

Hawk shook his head. "And you never will. Not officially, at least. Our team leader was a guy they called Chalice."

"Ah," Bear said.

Hawk made a sharp right turn and started back in the direction of their hotel. "In any event," he said, "tonight we meet our asset."

= THIRTY-SEVEN =

ASSET

Ciudad del Este, Paraguay
January 13, 2005

It was later that same evening when Bear and Hawk arrived at a Japanese-themed restaurant in the city. It was called Omari. Aside from its cuisine, an advantage of the establishment was that its tables were partitioned off by heavy drapery, affording its diners a degree of privacy. At least from prying eyes, if not necessarily from ears.

The Japanese hostess at the front of the house greeted them effusively and led them to their shrouded table where they found themselves seated across from a woman who was familiar - at least to one of them.

She smiled knowingly at Hawk.

"Eladio," she said.

"Vardah," he replied. "Good to see you again."

In truth, Hawk and Vardah had been in touch multiple times after their first interaction in Beirut, back in 1998. Over the course of the past eight years, she had become a registered asset of the Org, with Hawk as her occasional case officer. As such, she also became a Legal Permanent Resident, or Green Card holder, of the United States.

It had been eight years since their initial contact in Beirut. The passage of time had not disfavored her. True, some of her past glamor had faded and her features had sharpened just a bit. Nevertheless, the operative effect was to render her appearance as even more exotic than before.

"And this fine gentleman is called Bear," Hawk said as his partner settled into his chair.

"Bear," she smiled amicably.

"Vardah."

"And the role of the lovely Vardah in this adventure?" Bear asked.

"Her role," Hawk said, "will be to ensure that Hank Bayard, formerly of the United States Air Force, does not escape American justice."

Bear nodded approvingly and raised his glass. "Salud!"

"Salud," Hawk and Vardah responded approvingly.

= THIRTY-EIGHT =

HABIBI

Ciudad Del Este, Paraguay
January 17, 2005

It was a sleepy Monday morning. Hank Bayard, more lately known to the locals as Abu Saif, was alone in the shop. His wife was gone for her weekly shopping trip at the markets.

He was intrigued by a message that he had received over the weekend from a business contact, someone that he knew only as Hadi. All that he knew of this Hadi character was that he was a fellow money launderer. And that he appeared to be located somewhere in the Cayman Islands.

According to Hadi, Bayard was to expect a new depositor in his shop that very day. The depositor would be using a particular Koranic phrase as proof of their identity. Most importantly, the deposit was to be expedited as soon as it had been received. The recipient on the other side, Hadi emphasized, was someone of importance. Someone who was eager to see the transaction completed.

It was close to noon when the bell over the door jangled indicating the arrival of a visitor. Bayard looked up to see an Islamic woman, fully cloaked with a hijab over her head and a veil covering her face below the eyes. She was carrying a weighty leather satchel over her shoulder.

There was something vaguely familiar about the woman. A sort of tenuous familiarity. But he dismissed the thought.

"As-Salamu-Alaikum," he said by way of greeting.

"Salam," she replied flatly.

The woman placed her satchel on the countertop and snapped it open. Inside were bundles of Paraguayan guarani bills - the local currency.

Bayard glanced at the money and back at the woman.

"And do not mix the truth with falsehood," she recited. "Or conceal the truth while you know it."

It was the expected Koranic recognition phrase. The Surah Baqarah Ayat 42. This was Hadi's promised depositor.

There was something about her that was troublingly familiar. The voice. The demeanor.

"You," Bayard said slowly. "I seem to know you."

"Yes," the woman agreed. "You have known me... Both personally and, as they say, biblically." She loosened her veil and let it fall aside, exposing her face.

"You," Bayard said with a shock of recognition. "Vardah? Can you be ... Vardah?"

"Habibi," she said in reply. *Beloved.*

Several moments of stunned silence passed between them.

"I... I thought," he stammered. "I thought..."

"You thought what?... That I was dead?"

"Not dead. But..."

"No. Neither of us is dead. You are the one who left," she interrupted. "Suddenly. With no warning."

Bayard turned his eyes downward, in something akin to shame.

"Almost nine years gone by," she prodded. "Nine years, Hank."

"I had to leave," he said finally. "There were issues. Serious issues."

He looked back at her. "But I never forgot you. You were always in my heart."

"*Wa'ana kadhalik*," she said after a brief pause. *And me as well.*

Bayard was wordless.

"I imagine that you are surprised to see me."

"Surprised?" he repeated. His eyes reflexively darted to the doorway to ensure that they were alone. "That's putting it... mildly. But what happened with you?"

Vardah paused for a long moment. "In the past years my way of life in Beirut lost its meaning," she explained. "I fell into drugs. I considered ending my life. But then, the elder sister of my mother..."

"Your aunt," Bayard prodded.

"Yes. My aunt. Tharaa was her name. She was a religious woman. She found me and brought me back to life... And to Allah."

" *Al-Hamdulillah*," Bayard said.

"Yes," Vardah agreed. "Praise be to God."

Bayard reached for a bottle of water and took a long swig. "And so, why are you here now?" he asked at length.

"The same reason as you, as I understand it," she said.

Bayard continued to stare at her wordlessly.

"The Cause," she explained. "The struggle to defend our faith."

"On whose behalf?"

"You would know."

"On whose behalf?" he repeated.

Vardah hesitated. "*Muqawamah*," she said.

"The Resistance," Bayard repeated. "Hezbollah?"

"Hezbollah, yes, if I must say it aloud," she said. "They sent me to this area nearly a year ago."

"And only now..."

"And only now it was operationally necessary for me to contact you, among other hawaladars," she said, completing the thought.

Bayard was beginning to regain his presence of mind. "What is it that you need?"

"I need a hawaladar who can be trusted. And one who would agree to keep no records of this transaction."

"But why?"

"Because the recipient is a very special person whose identity must be protected. Even more than most."

"Let me have the money, Vardah, "Bayard said. "And I will make the transfer for you."

She slid the satchel full of guarani bills across the countertop and watched as he began to count it. Bayard stopped his counting when Vardah put both of her hands on his.

"I am now a woman of faith," she said, touching his cheek lightly with her fingertips, as she had done so many times in the past. "But I am still a woman.

= THIRTY-NINE =

ASSIGNATION

Ciudad Del Este, Paraguay
January 17, 2005

As soon as Vardah left the Cosas Electronicas shop, Hank Bayard set to work on making the transfer as agreed. In this case, it was a bit more complicated than his usual business activities. He had to navigate through two other trusted hawaladar contacts until he could identify a reliable end source in Geneva, Switzerland. Once notified to the Swiss counterpart that he was also reliable, Bayard pushed through the coded message that actuated the virtual movement of Vardah's funds.

In less than an hour, he received confirmation of the transaction from Europe. That completed, Bayard locked up his shop and left to deposit the cash in a bank account that he had established for such purposes. And to make plans for the evening.

* * *

Unbeknownst to Bayard, as he went about his business, an offshore SIGINT station monitored his financial transfer out of Paraguay. As planned, a similar intercept hub located in Bern, Switzerland, confirmed the arrival of the message. In the latter case, it was traced to the home of an expatriate Turkish florist in Geneva. Within hours, they noted the transfer of funds, now in the form of Swiss francs, to the bank account of yet another expatriate. The recipient account owner was named *Monsieur* J. A. Gauthier, a resident of the Eaux-Vives district of Geneva.

As US Intelligence authorities knew, 'Jules Andre Gauthier' was an alias for Javid Mokri, senior leader in the Iranian Supreme National Security Council.

Close to midnight, Washington time, a liaison officer at the National Security Agency called a secure line at the Org in McLean, Virginia. She confirmed to the duty analyst that the financial transaction had been completed as designed. That information was then conveyed to the team in Ciudad del Este, Paraguay. Loop closed.

* * *

That evening, Bayard advised his wife that he needed to meet with an important personage who was connected to the Hezbollah-related hawala business. Being an ostensibly obedient Muslim woman, Kalima did not question him. But she did have her suspicions, based upon his past behaviors. He was replicating for her, she feared, the unspoken life that she had left behind many years ago.

Bayard's tale was only half a lie. He was indeed going to a prearranged meeting with an important depositor - Vardah.

Bayard left home dressed in western clothing, jeans, a pullover shirt, and a light jacket against the threat of rain. No Muslim affiliations were apparent in this case. He drove northward across the city to a small tourist hotel near the National University. He checked into a room on the third floor and waited.

As he whiled away the time, he reflected on the developments that led him from the life of a normal patriotic American citizen to that of a Muslim activist in Paraguay.

Bayard joined the US Air Force fresh out of high school in Clovis, New Mexico. He had been eager to make a career of the service, pinning his hopes on becoming a member of an aircrew with its added attractions of adventure and flight pay. Those hopes, however, foundered when he failed to meet the strict requirements of the flight physical exams. He was nonetheless successful in assignment to his secondary choice in the Intelligence career field.

Early on, the young Airman had taken an interest in the history and culture of the Middle East, going so far as to dabble in Arabic language lessons and Islamic philosophy on his own time. He came to sympathize with what he saw as a region of largely oppressed and exploited people.

Even as a teenager in the 1980's, Bayard had followed the global news with a curiosity that marked him apart from his peers. Of special interest to him was the Iraqi aggression against their fellow Muslims in Iran. In his view, the Iranians were struggling to defend their land and religion against the secular threat posed by Baghdad.

He was to become more directly involved with Iraqi matters in 1990, when Saddam Hussein invaded Kuwait, initiating the Gulf War. Although the focus of the Gulf War was on Kuwait and Iraq, Bayard never set foot in either country. Instead, he was assigned as an Intelligence Specialist with the headquarters of the 14th Air Division (USCENTAF), located in Riyadh, Saudi Arabia. What he saw in the land that was sarcastically referred to as "the Magic Kingdom", offended his sensibilities. Especially in terms of extravagant wealth and hypocritical social policies.

He arrived at what was to be his last posting with the Air Force, the US Embassy in Beirut, Lebanon, in mid-1995. By that point in his life, he was beginning to question the logic of US foreign policy in the Muslim world.

Several months after his arrival, Bayard was approached off-duty by an elderly local man who claimed to have heard about him from others. The man introduced himself as Yaqub, from the village of Nahleh in the Bekaa Valley.

Yaqub complimented Bayard on his political acumen, social awareness, and growing religious convictions. As a gift, he provided the American with a few books and pamphlets to enhance his further study.

Contrary to established security regulations, Bayard did not file a foreign contact report of his new-found Lebanese friend.

It was only after their third meeting, this time over dinner in a secluded establishment, that the kindly Yaqub suggested that if Bayard truly wanted to help the people of the region, he could provide a means to do so. Bayard was interested.

And then there was Vardah. What started as a brief fling with a call girl, or a 'courtesan', as she preferred to identify, bloomed into a relationship of a more serious nature. Despite his feelings for her, even she remained ignorant of his plans when he walked out of the Embassy one evening in October of 1996.

Several blocks away from the Embassy, Bayard reached a point that Yaqub had previously described. There, as expected, an unknown man wordlessly placed him in the back of a car and slipped a hood over his head. From there he was transported to a village in the Bekaa. And so began his association with Hezbollah.

* * *

Within an hour there was a tentative knock at the door. He opened it after a brief hesitation and greeted his visitor. Like himself, Vardah was now garbed in western clothing, a canvas bag slung over her shoulder. And she was as alluring as ever.

Pushing the door shut, Bayard gave her a chaste kiss on the cheek and stepped back to regard her more fully. "You are... still beautiful," he offered. "Or is that something awkward to say?"

Vardah pulled him closer once again and kissed him fully on the lips. "Not awkward, habibi," she smiled. "Endearing. After all of these years."

"All these years," he repeated.

Reaching into her shoulder bag, she pulled out a dark green bottle and held it briefly aloft.

"Wine?" he remarked.

She nodded. "There are no judgmental people of the faith here to watch us," she said. "Are there?"

"None."

"Like the old days then," she said, uncorking the bottle. "Back home."

After another lingering kiss, she placed the bottle on a coffee table and straightened her blouse. "But first," she said. "To business habibi. The money of my backers?"

Bayard sat onto the couch next to Vardah.

"Settled," he said. "But not without some issues. It took a bit of effort to locate some new contacts who could be trusted to move the message along."

"But?'

"But I was successful," he said. "The recipient should have the money in his account by now."

"My hero," she laughed. "You deserve a reward."

"If you say so."

Vardah eased back on the couch. "Let me reward you then, habibi. My love."

Giving vent to his long-repressed memories of the most exciting love of his life, Bayard took her in a close embrace. "I can't believe that you appeared today," he whispered. "God is truly good. I can't lose you again."

"No," she breathed. "You never will."

It was close to dawn when Bayard reluctantly left for home.

= FORTY =

NOTICIAS

US Embassy
Asuncion, Paraguay
January 18, 2005

It was late morning when Regional Security Officer Brian Quigley received the message that he had a visitor down at Post One. It was his liaison pal, the Marine said, Colonel Olivera of the National Police. He asked his Office Management Specialist, Jake, to go down to Post One and escort the good *Coronel* up to the office.

In truth, Quigley was already well aware of the news that the PNP officer was bringing. But, ever striving to be the good diplomat/security official, he was more than willing to play the game of the receptive host. Scrambling just a bit, and with the help of one of his assistants, he was able to gin up some sweetened coffee and Danishes when the not entirely unexpected guest made his way up to the RSO office spaces.

Before long, the personable and ever sociable Olivera appeared at the door.

"*Mi Coronel*," Quigley said, rising from his chair to embrace him. "Always good to see you."

"*Igualmente*," Olivera said with a smile. "*Muy amable*."

As they sat down to sip their coffee and snack on the pastries, Olivera provided Quigley with details as to what had transpired that morning in Ciudad del Este.

According to the report that he had just received, that very morning a PNP team executed a raid in Ciudad del Este on the shop called Cosas Electronicas. Awaiting outside but not permitted to enter or otherwise participate in the operation, were representatives of Quigley's own Diplomatic Security Service, as well as the embassy's Legal Attaché's office, otherwise known as the FBI.

Quigley set his cup down and leaned forward. "So, what happened?"

"*Bueno,*" Olivera said. "Just before the opening time, the PNP team entered the shop. Only this man Bayard and his wife were inside. The team moved quickly. There was no resistance. No violence."

Quigley nodded. "How did they react?"

Olivera glanced at his notes. "This Bayard, they said, almost seemed to be relieved to have been caught. *La Signora,* on the other hand, appeared to be shocked and angry. They said that she glared at the team with hate as they went through the search procedure. But she did nothing to interfere."

The RSO reached for his own notepad. He would need to be sending a cable to DS Headquarters shortly. "Was the wife arrested as well?"

"*Si. Los dos.*"

"Where are they being held now?" he asked.

"The *Carcel Regional* in del Este," Olivera said. "Your embassy, of course, will be asking for his extradition to America."

"Um-hmm," Quigley said, jotting on his pad. "And when do you think that might be?"

"Not long," Olivera replied. Two weeks to three weeks. Maybe more. Maybe less."

"That's pretty quick."

Olivera shook his head. "Your Abu Saif gentleman has gained little love among officialdom here. And his Hezbollah connections have even less."

"I am aware," Quigley agreed.

"Yes," the Coronel continued. "Our neighbors in Argentina suffered twice from their plots. I speak of their 1992 bombing of the Israeli Embassy in Buenos Aires, followed two years later by the bombing of the Jewish Cultural Center in the same city. More than 200 souls were killed between the two events. And more than 500 injured."

"Yes."

"And so, *los Argentinos* declared Hezbollah to be a terrorist organization. And we in Paraguay followed their example. We have no desire to have similar experiences with these bastards."

"Therefore?" Quigley prompted.

"Bayard is no *Paraguayo*. In fact, he entered the country on a false Canadian passport. He has no claims here at all. You can have him, I am told."

Quigley put his pen down and reached for the coffee cup. "We'll take him."

= FORTY-ONE =

COMPOS MENTIS

Alexandria, Virginia
May 12, 2005

WFO SAC Jake Kaczmar was paying a mid-morning visit to the US Attorney's Office on Courthouse Square in Alexandria. But he was not alone, having been accompanied by Leah Chaikin and her supervisor, Bobbi. They were cooling their collective heels in a conference room while awaiting the arrival of the AUSA who was handing the Henry Bayard case, Guillaume Sanon.

As it developed, Colonel Olivera, of the PNP in Paraguay, was a bit off in his assessment of the extradition process. While Bayard did not object to the request, a small local human rights group did. Claiming that he was a victim of an oppressive colonial power, they filed a legal brief to hold him in country.

The government in Asuncion, however, would have none of it. They denied the brief and allowed the US Marshals Service to take custody of Bayard and transport him back to the United States. Specifically, to the federal jurisdiction of the Eastern District of Virginia, or EDVA, in Alexandria.

While they waited, Bobbi pushed a newspaper clipping across the table to Kaczmar. "Guess you heard of this?" she asked.

The clipping was from that Monday's New York Times, and it was about Yellowcake. It seemed that the

Government of the Islamic Republic of Iran had just admitted to converting 37 tons of raw uranium - Yellowcake - into a gas known as uranium tetrafluoride or, more simply, UF4. As the article noted, this was a critical step in the enrichment of uranium. That was itself was a progression toward the development of a nuclear weapon. The Iranians, nevertheless, asserted that this was only for the peaceful use of nuclear energy. The US Government, and more so the Government of Israel, had their doubts.

"This says that it happened last November," Kaczmar observed.

"Yes," Bobbi agreed. "That's Iran. And Iran is Hezbollah."

"And Hezbollah is Bayard," Leah added.

At that point the door was pushed open and AUSA Sanon entered, juggling a coffee in one hand and a folder of papers in the other.

"*Bonjour* everyone" he said. "Sorry to keep you waiting. Case conference on another guy ran longer than was expected." The Prosecutor's faint Haitian accent was still detectable despite his many years of life in the States.

The DS agents smiled, mumbled their acknowledgements, and shifted their attention to him.

Dropping into a chair, Sanon placed the coffee cup on the tabletop safely away from himself and proceeded to open the file folder. "So, the other news that we have today is this..." He paused.

"Yes?" Kaczmar prodded.

"The news is that Mister Henry Alan Bayard, also known as Thomas William Adkins, also known as Abu Saif, also known on whatever name he used on that Canadian passport in Paraguay, has flipped. He has now agreed to plead guilty and become a cooperating witness for the US Government."

"Wow," Leah exclaimed quietly.

"And why did he do that?" Kaczmar asked.

"He has, I guess you would say, found religion."

"He already had religion," Leah interjected. "Thanks to his friends in Hezbollah."

Sanon nodded. "But I refer to the religion found in 18 USC. The US criminal code. Specifically, Title 18 USC 2339B."

"Which is?" said Bobbi.

"Providing Material Support to Designated Terrorist Organizations," he said. "The penalties include a fine and up to 20 years in prison, or both. However," he continued, "That prison term could be extended to life if anyone was killed as a result of the crime."

"Which is quite likely, given the Hezbollah ties," Bobbi said.

"Not to mention our original 1542 Passport Fraud charges," Kaczmar said.

"Of course not," Sanon agreed. "That's what brought us to this party."

"And Bayard's plea is going to hold up under scrutiny?" Kaczmar pressed.

Sanon nodded. "We did a psych evaluation of him. The doc's judgment is that he is *compos mentis*. In other words, mastery of one's own mind. Of sound mind and able to make his own decisions."

"What about his desertion charges from the military?" Bobbi asked.

"Yes," Sanon agreed. "The Air Force is very interested in getting ahold of him for his unapproved departure from the DAO in Beirut. But we in Justice have the first call on him. They can have him next."

"So where do we go from here?" Leah asked.

Sanon took a sip of coffee, daintily replaced it on the table and folded his hands. "Let's see what he has to give us."

= FORTY-TWO =

CHIEF OPS

McLean, Virginia
August 8, 2005

Bart Landau appeared in the office of Lonnie Mills early on that Monday morning. He was carrying a portion of the JADE SORCERER file along with him.

"Bart," Mills said, looking up from his papers. "Iran?" he speculated. "Whenever I see you, I think *Iran*."

"*Salaam*," Landau replied with more than a hint of sarcasm, placing his right hand over his heart and dipping his head. He dropped into a proffered chair and placed the file folder on Mill's desktop.

"And this is?"

Landau crossed his legs. "Bayard. Henry Alan Bayard."

Mills nodded, "Yes. Also known as Abu Saif. I *do* read the reports. As I recall, he's gone from deserter/defector to Hezbollah asset, and now to Government witness... Do I have that about right?"

"Indeed," Landau nodded. "He's been a good guy and then a bad guy. And now he's pretending to be a good guy again."

"Pretending?"

"In my humble opinion, yes."

"Great. So, he's now back in US custody, where he belongs."

"That he is," Landau agreed.

"And what does that have to do with us?"

Landau tapped a finger on the case folder. "Actually, there may be a way to play this development back against the Iranian target. In support of Hawk's SORCERER operation."

Mills pulled the folder closer to him. "How so?"

Landau shifted in his seat, stretching his neck from side to side. "Okay. While the Iranians don't have formal diplomatic relations with the United States," he said, "they actually *do* have an official presence here."

"Is that the case?"

"Technically, it is. Just as we are represented by the Swiss Embassy in Tehran, the Iranians have an Interest Section located within the Pakistani Embassy right here in Washington. At the moment, it's being run by a guy named Ali Jazini Dorcheh. Has a background in Iranian police circles, so no doubt a hard-liner."

"What else would he be? And?"

"And, the Iranians just had a presidential election over there a few days ago. The new guy is named Mahmoud Ahmadinejad. He's a former mayor of Tehran. Former provincial governor of Kurdistan. Proponent of their nuclear weapons program. Maybe a former member of the Revolutionary Guards. Maybe a former Basiji member. Maybe even one of the hostage takers who took over our embassy in '79."

Mills cocked his head. "Basiji?'

"Paramilitary militia."

"Wonderful. So, how does Bayard fit into this?"

"Well, as a happy coincidence, the FBI has an in with someone over there at the Interest Section," Landau said. "In FBI terms, it's called a Controlled Human Source, or a CHS... No idea whether the Source is an Iranian or Paki staff member, but there he is. And I'm sure that the CHS is a *he*."

Mills nodded agreeably. "Okay, so what's the plan?"

"The plan," Landau said, "would be to leak to the FBI source in the Interests Section the Bayard is not only becoming a cooperating witness with the Government, but that he knows something else."

"That being?"

"That Bayard is telling us that the Israelis have a high-ranking source of their own in Tehran. And we could float a name of our own."

"And that goes back to Hawk's man in Tehran..."

"And the Iranians do the rest," Landau sad, completing the thought.

"I'll run it past JD," Mills said, pushing the folder back across the desk. "But I'm thinking, let's do it."

= FORTY-THREE =

AZADI MUSEUM

Tehran, Iran
September 14, 2005

It was late in the afternoon that Tuesday. Despite the hazy heat of a pending autumn, one could still catch a view of the fabled Mount Damavand off to the northeast of the city.

Sometimes known as the Roof of Persia, the volcanic Damavand peak, part of the Alborz Mountain range, is the highest point of elevation in all of Iran. According to legend, an ancient serpent king named Zahhak once ruled there for a thousand years, routinely sacrificing his subjects to feed his serpents.

That was until a character named Kaveh the Blacksmith led a revolution, ultimately conquering and beheading the evil Zahhak for his cruelty. Even today, each March on the Spring Equinox, Kaveh's victory is celebrated by Iranians as *Nowruz*, or the New Day. The Persian New Year.

Regardless of fables, fairy tales, or legends, there was more than enough cruelty still awash in the lands below the mountaintop. More than to suffice for years to come.

Hawk had been in the city for two days now. He had flown in from Vienna, landing at the capital's Imam Khomeini International Airport. He was traveling under his French-Canadian pseudonym of Etienne Alban. This was facilitated by a Canadian passport which identified his place of birth as Trois-Rivieres in Quebec province.

The process of backstopping the passport was the least of Hawk's worries. The book was a genuine document, issued by the Canadian authorities as part of the *Five Eyes* arrangement.

Five Eyes was an intelligence sharing arrangement between the United States and Canada, as well as the other English-speaking nations of the United Kingdom, New Zealand, and Australia. As a result, the Canadian agency then known as Passport Canada, agreed to document the American Org operative for this particular mission.

Hawk had stepped into the lion's den to make contact with his MOIS agent, Shahriar Parviz. The purpose of the visit was to convey the supposed compromising Bayard information to his contact. And, hopefully, to the higher powers of the government.

Hawk stopped to gaze at the largely indecipherable offerings of a newsstand. With a degree of nodding and finger pointing, he was able to purchase a Farsi language newspaper. Upon receiving it, he deftly slipped an envelope from his jacket pocket and folded it into the paper.

As he did so, he caught sight of the stocky figure of Escobar ambling along the sidewalk toward him.

Hawk had requested that the Bosniaks be available as his covering team in Tehran. This was both due to his confidence in their capabilities as well as the fact that they could easily recognize Parviz from their past interaction in Dushanbe. Both had entered Tehran from East European countries on Bosnian passports.

Escobar straddled up alongside Hawk, looking at the incomprehensible print of the Farsi newspapers. "He's there," Escobar murmured. "Now. And alone."

"Zlatko?" Hawk asked.

"Still down there with him. All is clear."

Hawk nodded and continued on toward the destination. Escobar kept watch on his progress from behind.

Looming ahead of Hawk in the near distance was the impressive national monument called the Azadi Tower.

The Azadi Tower was a 140-foot square-topped construct, with flowing white marble wings arching from on either side. It was commissioned in 1966 by Mohammad Reza Pahlavi, the last Shah of Iran. The Shah's intent had been to commemorate the 2,500th anniversary of the Persian empire, of which he was the latest sovereign. Ironically, the project was to predate the overthrow of his own government by a scant 13 years.

And after the fall of the Shah came the current regime, the Islamic Republic of Iran. The country that had once been a reliable, if non-treaty, ally of the United States was now an implacable enemy.

Hawk entered the Azadi complex and went down the stairs and into the museum crypt. After meandering around for a few moments, he saw the angular Zlatko Piric. Although he made no overt sign of recognition, Zlatko pulled out a handkerchief to dab at his eyes. Cleared to make contact.

Further along the corridor amidst the displays of pottery, gold, and paintings, was his contact, Shahriar Parviz.

After a few moments of apparently studying the various *objets d'art*, Hawk casually sidled up beside Parviz. The latter was gazing at a display of an ancient clay tablet with a mass of indecipherable lettering carved into it.

"Shahriar," he said quietly by means of greeting.

"Etienne," Parviz replied, not taking his eyes off of the display. "Good to see you again."

"De meme," was the reply. Likewise.

"Interesting," Hawk murmured, peering more intently at the clay tablet. "Just what are we looking at?"

Parviz cocked his head. "How to explain? ... It is a document, probably a government document, that is thousands of years old. Maybe as much as 5,000 years. It was found in Susa."

"Susa?"

"It's a place in the Zagros Mountains, in the southwest of our country," Parviz explained. "Near what is now the Iraqi border. Back then, it was the capital of the Persian king, Darius the Great."

Hawk shook his head. "I'm not familiar with him."

"His son was Xerxes the First. He was the man who invaded Greece through the famous pass at Thermopylae in 480 BC," Parviz explained. The Three Hundred Spartans at the Hot Gates and all of that."

"With that, I am familiar," Hawk replied.

"And what, my friend, what brings you into the modern hot gates of Tehran today?" Parviz continued softly, not removing his gaze from the encased clay tablet before them.

“To provide you with what may well be career-enhancing information,” Hawk said, placing the folded newspaper on the glass counter before them.

“And what is the nature of this information?”

“A member of the Postal Union has been arrested in South America,” Hawk said, using their mutually agreed-upon term for Hezbollah. “He is now cooperating with the Americans. And they with us.”

Parviz digested this for a moment. “And what is the Union man’s area of expertise.”

“Money. Financial transactions.”

“And?”

Hawk shot a glance in Zlatko’s direction. Again, he was given an all-clear signal.

“The Union man has implicated your colleague as a recipient of some of these funds,” Hawk continued. “To his detriment. And possibly to your advantage.”

“I see,” Parviz said. It was obvious that they were discussing Javier Mokri of the Supreme National Security Council and a strong contender to be the next head of the MOIS.

Hawk placed the folded newspaper on the glass counter in front of the encased clay tablet. "There is a thumb drive inside of that," he said. "It should provide you with all of the information you need to begin an enquiry into the other gentleman."

"I see."

"The thumb drive is password-protected," Hawk continued. "It will be provided to you separately."

"Understood."

"Then that concludes our business. We will be in touch," Hawk said. "Be very careful with the information."

"Unnecessary to say," Parviz replied. "Travel safely."

= FORTY-FOUR =

ELAHIYEH

Tehran, Iran
September 16, 2005

Javed Mokri was spending the late afternoon relaxing at his residence in the upscale neighborhood of Elahiyeh in northern Tehran. Friday prayers had finished earlier and his workday at the offices of the Supreme National Security Council (SNSC) had concluded as well.

Yet it was not time so much to relax. Perhaps more a moment to sit back and enjoy his recent successes.

Having married fairly late in life, the gray-bearded Mokri delighted in his two young children, a boy and a girl, who were even then cavorting happily in his study. Sitting at his desk, he turned his attention to a series of reports that had just appeared at the SNSC that morning.

Mokri nodded appreciatively to the children's nanny as she placed a tray containing a ceramic pot of steaming hot tea and a small bowl of sugar cubes on his desk. That done, she shepherded the children out of the study.

As a degree of peaceful silence having thankfully returned, Mokri turned his attention to the sheaf of papers on his end table.

The information contained in the reports was less a revelation than a celebration of his own efforts in work against what the propagandists called the Little Satan - Israel.

For the past several months Iran had been actively involved in the efforts to remove the Israelis from the area known as the Gaza Strip. From Mokri's perspective, these efforts were heavily involved with his primary regional clients on behalf of the Iranian state, Hamas and Hezbollah.

Earlier in the year, the Syrian President Bashar al-Assad had announced the withdrawal of all Syrian forces from Lebanon. It was not a concern for Mokri. Bashar was a trusted ally of Iran, even more reliable than his father Hafez had been. Under Bashar's rule, Syria provided a land connection for the movement of Iranian weapons to their proxy of Hezbollah in Lebanon.

The same could hardly be said for Israel.

The Israelis had occupied Gaza since the 1967 Six-Day War. Their first Jewish settlements in the area were established thirty-five years earlier, in 1970.

Thirty-five years of occupation, Mokri reflected. *A travesty by any comparison. One that has now been corrected.*

After years of struggle, the Israelis had finally agreed to withdraw from Gaza. This meant the pullout of all Israeli military as well as all of the thousands of civilian settlers in the area. The unlikely driving force behind the withdrawal was the current Prime Minister, Ariel Sharon.

Unlikely because Sharon was a hardline member of the conservative Likud Party. A former IDF General, and former Defense Minister, he earned the moniker of "*Butcher of Beirut*" after the 1982 massacre at the Sabra and Shatila Palestinian refugee camp during the Israeli invasion of Lebanon. The incident cost Sharon his post, but not his career in politics.

The move was met with heavy opposition in Jerusalem, including members of his own Likud, although the leftists of the Labor Party heartily supported the decision.

Although the original deadline had been set for August the 15th, the actual pullout was finally accomplished just four days earlier, September 12th.

Not the least of Mokri's satisfaction was the fact that control of Gaza and its people had now transferred to the governance of one of his proxies - Hamas.

Javed Mokri poured himself another cup of tea and toasted to his own success.

= FORTY-FIVE =

CHS

Falls Church, Virginia
September 24, 2005

Special Agent Ronny Chu glanced at his wristwatch. It was half past noon on a dismal Saturday in the Washington, DC metropolitan area. He was parked along Leesburg Pike in Falls Church, an independent polity situated between the Northern Virginia counties of Arlington and Fairfax.

Across the highway and down the road a bit was a leafy square that partially concealed a mosque called the Dar al-Hijrah Islamic Center. The mosque was well known to the FBI. Its past congregants included two of the 9/11 al-Qaeda hijackers, Hani Hanjour and Nawaf al-Hazmi, as well as the New Mexican-born Anwar al-Alwaki. The latter had been an Imam at the mosque until his departure for Yemen the previous year. His activities there were still of interest and were being closely monitored by the US intelligence community.

After some twenty minutes of further waiting, a tan Volkswagen Beetle pulled out of the mosque's parking lot and made a right, heading northwest along the Pike.

Chu keyed his radio as he watched the VW pass by him. "He's out," he said. "Alone. And moving."

"Copy," crackled a reedy voice on the speaker.

"I copy," chimed in a second voice.

"Rog," said a third.

Chu watched as three unmarked FBI cars slipped out of their separate commercial parking lots and began to trail the VW as it motored up the Pike. These were the watchers of the SSG, the Bureau's Special Surveillance Group.

Within a half hour, one of the voices came back up on the channel. "Okay. He's stopped at the location," the voice said. "And clean. No followers observed."

"Agree. Confirm clean," came a second SSG voice.

"Great," Chu replied. "Give us a few minutes and then head into the site."

"Got it."

* * *

The tan VW was parked in the expansive lot of the Eden Center.

The Eden Center was primarily a Vietnamese business shopping area. Named after a former Saigon shopping mall, it proudly flew a large yellow banner with three horizontal red bands over the entrance. It was the old flag of South Vietnam. The occupants of the Center were flaunting their allegiance, despite what realities might actually exist back in the homeland.

As Chu clambered out of his car, the occupant of the VW also exited and followed him to the randomly selected Vietnamese restaurant. As they entered, he saw one of the SSG men sitting at a corner table and spooning into a freshly arrived bowl of *pho* noodle soup. The other two operatives remained outside, keeping watch on the comings and goings of the parking lot.

Chu and the VW driver, Danush was his name, settled into a table and ordered a pair of *banh mi* sandwiches.

Danush was an Iranian citizen who was born in the northwestern city of Tabriz. For the past couple of years, he had been employed as a Passport Officer at the Iranian Interest Section. The Iranian Section was, by diplomatic agreement, housed in the Pakistani Embassy in Washington. Within the last year, however, Arash had become a heavily vetted Controlled Human Source for the counterintelligence people of the FBI. Chu was his handler.

The two made small talk until the food arrived. That done, the conversation quietly turned to business as they began to eat.

"And so?" Danush finally asked.

"You," Chu said. "Is everything okay with you?"

Danush nodded. "All is well," he said. "If not, I think that you might be the first to know."

"We have heard nothing of concern."

"That is comforting," Danush said. "Then what is the reason for this unplanned meeting?'

Chu paused as a server moved further away from the table. "We have information that needs to find its way into Tehran."

"Tehran."

"At the highest possible levels."

Chu casually produced a padded envelope and left it on the table. It contained a folder of money as well as the falsified intelligence material. The latter, which was known to the older hands as *chickenfeed*, was attributed to Bayard's alleged disclosures.

"The details are in there," he said. "As well as your stipend."

Danush slipped the envelope across the table and into his jacket pocket. "And how do I explain the origins of this ... mysterious information?"

"The ISI," Chu answered, referring to the Inter-Services Intelligence service, the primary Pakistani spy agency.

"We know that the Pakistani Deputy Political Officer is actually an ISI operative working in a covered position," Chu continued. "You can imply, or say, that the information came from him. But caution the Iranians not to pursue the point, so as not to damage your supposed relationship with him."

Danush nodded his head and took another bite of his sandwich. "That might work," he muttered.

"And if not," Chu added, "to quote yourself, you will be the first to know."

= FORTY-SIX =

THE SECRETARY

Tehran, Iran
October 5, 2005

Ali Ardeshir Larijani, the freshly appointed Secretary of the Supreme National Security Council (SNSC), pulled off his glasses, dropping them carelessly on his desk. He rubbed his eyes wearily. So many projects and proposals to review. So much responsibility.

The SNSC was, as specified by the constitution, Iran's highest decision-making authority for national security affairs. Its elite membership included the President himself, as well the Judiciary and Parliament heads, plus the various chiefs of the intelligence and military branches. And other personages as needed.

Two months into the new position, despite his personal history, he was still grappling with the various machinations of the Council.

The Iraqi-born Larijani was no stranger to power. He was previously a Brigadier General in the Islamic Revolutionary Guard Corps, or the IRGC. Established in 1979, in the early days following the Revolution, the IRGC evolved into a highly powerful, and highly feared, organization within the Iranian structure. Preeminent among the Iranian armed forces, its operations included links with proxy groups in Lebanon, Iraq, Syria, Yemen, and of course the Palestinian territories.

Subsequent to his time with the IRGC, Larijani held the less dramatic, though influential, post of head of the Republic of Iran Broadcasting Service. Most recently, he worked as the security advisor to the Supreme Leader himself, the Ayatollah Ali Khamenei. And now...

There was a light, respectful tapping on his office door. This would be the unexpected last-minute appointment. Larijani replaced his glasses and cleared his throat. "Come in," he said wearily.

As the other entered, Larijani recognized him to be one the senior MOIS officers in his entourage. "Parviz, isn't it?" he ventured.

"Yes sir," the visitor said. "Shahriar Parviz. MOIS. Please excuse me for interrupting your day. I realize that your time is valuable."

"Yes, yes," Larijani said, nodding his head. "What is it?"

"May I sit?"

"Please sit," Larijani replied with just a hint of irritation. "Again. What is the point of your visit?"

Parviz settled into a chair in front of the desk. He unlocked and unzipped a leather folder that he held in his lap. Admittedly, he felt some trepidation with this ploy, knowing he was accusing a senior officer of being an agent of Israeli intelligence when he himself was an agent of what he believed to be the French intelligence service.

"Sir, I appreciate the demands on your schedule. I would not intrude if it were not a matter of importance."

Larijani waved an impatient hand. "Go on."

"I am afraid that I have information regarding a serious threat to our Republic."

"What type of threat?" Larijani asked, his interest deepening a bit.

"Espionage," Parviz said. "There is, apparently, an Israeli spy among us."

Larijani frowned. "And why not send this though the usual channels to me?' he asked. "Instead of... Of this?"

Parviz produced the first of several documents from his folder. "Because, sir, " he said. "The suspect is one of your deputies here at the Council."

"Impossible," Larijani said. Then, after a reconsidered pause, "Who are you saying that it is?"

"Mokri," Parviz said. "Javed Mokri. A man who is still operating with the highest security clearances of the Republic."

Larijani pondered that for a moment.

"This man is a trusted deputy," he said at last. "A man with the confidence of the President. What is the basis of this charge?'

Parviz nodded and produced another document from his folder. "There have been several transfers of funds, four to be exact, from a financial expediter that we have used before. He is in George Town, the Cayman Islands. The funds traveled from the Caymans to an account in Geneva, Switzerland. These transfers occurred between last November and this September."

"And?"

A third document came from the folder and was placed on the desktop. "We had another expediter working in Ciudad del Este, Paraguay. Connected primarily with the Lebanese forces," Parviz continued, referring to Hezbollah. "He was also making transfers to this account in Geneva. Not an account of ours however. A private account."

"You said that *we had* another expediter."

Parviz nodded, "This Paraguay man is actually an American. He left their military when he was assigned to Beirut and came over to us. Unfortunately, they arrested him in January and took him back to the States."

"Yes?"

"And, according to our source at the Pakistani Embassy in Washington, this American has agreed to cooperate with the authorities. He is providing them with information that he has pertaining to our operations in the region."

"Can this American be dealt with? Silenced?"

"Uncertain," Parviz said. "He is in custody there. Under close supervision."

"Or for now at least," Larijani noted.

"In any event, "Parviz continued, "This American stated that he was sending money to this same account in Geneva. And that he believed

that some of the intermediaries delivering the cash to him appeared to be Jews."

"Jews?"

"Appeared to be Jews. He said."

"And lastly," Parviz said, introducing his final document. "We have a man in Damascus who is integral to our resources in the Bekaa Valley. He reported that a captured, and later rescued, source of ours believes overhearing idle talk to the effect that that the Israelis commenting about an agent that they have here in Tehran."

"Do we have a name on this account in Switzerland?" Larijani asked.

Parviz paused to consult a notebook, more for dramatic effect than for information. "Jules Andre Gauthier was the name on the Swiss account, sir." he said.

"What is the significance of that name?"

Parviz effected a sigh. "The Gauthier name has been used before in the past by Mokri for work purposes. Among others."

Larijani shuffled through the papers on his desk. "Would that be wise of Mokri to use a known identity for a private account with the Israelis?"

"If I may," Parviz said. "Within the ranks, Javed Mokri has a reputation for a rather extreme level of self-confidence. Coupled with some recklessness. It's what has made him successful so far."

"I see."

There were several long moments of silence as the Secretary digested the information.

"Alright, Larijani said, assembling the papers into a neat stack. "Thank you for bringing this information to my attention. I will consider the implications and take action if needed. You may go now."

Parviz rose, nodded and latched onto his empty leather folder. "Secretary," he said.

= FORTY-SEVEN =

STATUS UPDATE

Wilmington, Delaware
October 21, 2005

Chalice was spending the weekend at the Delaware home of Tas, his daughter and only child. Her actual name, Tasanee, was Thai for *a beautiful view.* She was the sole product of Chalice's failed marriage with her Thai mother, Somchai. The marriage was one to which Somchai's father had never given his approval. A retired General in the Thai Army with certain xenophobic views, he saw no value in the marriage of his only daughter to an American Army Warrant Officer, which Chalice was at the time. Regardless of the relationships, Tas was a refutation of that view.

Following Chalice's divorce, Tas was raised by her Thai mother in both Thailand and the US. After weighing her options in either country, she opted to pursue a nursing career with the Veterans' Administration in the United States.

After his discharge from the hospital the previous year, Chalice spent the majority of August there at his daughter's condo. Now he was back for a visit. And, for a meeting with the Org.

Chalice was polishing off the last crumbs of the desert as Tas set a cup of coffee in front of him. "Great stuff, Tas," he said. "You're a good cook."

"Learned from the best," she said, taking a seat with her own coffee.

"Not from me, though."

"No," she smiled.

"Anyhow," he continued. "Congrats on your promotion at the VA."

"Night Shift Nursing Supervisor. Not so very glamorous."

Chalice shrugged. "It's a step in the right direction. They like you. As they should."

Tas demurred, stirring some sweetener into her own coffee. "Tell me about The Dream again," she said.

The Dream.

It was a longstanding family tale. Bordering on obsession.

"Well, As I told you many times," Chalice began. "When I was a small boy, I had dreams of my Corsican grandfather visiting me."

"Yes."

"It happened several times. He visited me in my sleep to describe his home back in Corsica," Chalice said. "It was in a village called Figari. It's located on the southern end of the island. The people there were primarily wine producers. They cultivated vineyards dating as far back as back as to the days of the Romans. Supposedly as far as five hundred years before Christ."

"Yep. Even older than you."

"In the dream," he continued, "he took time to show me around the village and the surrounding fields. It was beautiful. Peaceful. Some place you would want to see."

"And?"

"Later, many years later, on one of my work trips to the region, I was able to take time off to go to Corsica and visit Figari. It was exactly as he described it."

"But?" Tas prodded with a knowing smile.

Chalice nodded. "But. I never actually met my grandfather. He died when I was an infant."

"Or so you claim to remember," she chided.

"And so, I claim."

Their age-old reverie/debate was interrupted by a light tapping on the door.

'That's him?" she asked.

"Most likely."

Tas went to the door and, after glancing through the peephole, opened it to see a middle-aged man standing there with a leather satchel slung over his shoulder.

"You must be Chalice's daughter," the visitor said.

"I am. And you are?"

"Bart Landau," the visitor said. "I work with your dad."

"I feel for you then," Tas chided. "But come on in. You're expected."

Chalice rose to greet him as well, shaking his hand. "Bart," he said. It's been a while."

"A long while," Landau agreed.

As Landau and Chalice chatted, Tas cleared the table and picked up her own bag. "I'm sure that you boys have stuff to talk about, but I'm off to work," she said.

"Kay," Chalice said. "Love you."

"Love you, too," she replied, closing the door behind her.

Landau made a production of arranging himself at the dinner table. That done, he produced his satchel, opened it, and withdrew a bottle of whiskey. "Got any glasses around here?" he asked.

"Is this a briefing or a celebration?" Chalice asked, rising from the table and fetching two glasses from the kitchen cabinet.

"A bit of both, I'd say."

Producing a corkscrew from the satchel, Landau stripped the foil from the bottle top and proceeded to twist the screw into the cork.

"What is that?" Chalice asked, sitting back down at the table.

"Irish whiskey," Landau said, popping the cork out theatrically. He poured out two generous dollops into the glasses. "A brand called *Writers Tears*."

Chalice took a sip. "Never heard of it."

"Me neither," Landau said. "Until a barkeep at an Irish pub on Columbia Pike in Arlington introduced me to it." He took a sip himself. "*'You'll do no better'*, the barkeep said. And he was right."

Chalice carefully placed his empty glass back onto the tabletop and tapped it expectantly on the rim. "And so?" he asked.

Landau poured in another splash for the both of them and pulled a few pages of classified documents from the satchel. "A quick status update on your case," he said. "And then I'll leave you to your free time."

"Go on."

Landau stretched his neck in anticipation. "So, as we know, the event that ended in your shooting there in San Juan was an attempt on behalf of the MOIS to kidnap an American Intelligence Officer. Most likely to take him back to Iran. Not especially you yourself."

"Okay. But why?"

Landau shrugged. "Reasons unknown. Maybe for political goals. A show trial to elicit international sympathy. Or maybe to hold out for a prisoner swap somewhere further down the road."

"Probably the latter," Chalice guessed.

"Hmmm."

"But why in Puerto Rico, of all places?"

Landau grimaced. "Ah, well. When you think *Puerto Rico*, do you think *Iran*?"

"Not really."

"Well then."

"So, what's happening?"

Landau cleared his throat and repositioned his glass on the tabletop. "Looks like the operation against Mr. Mokri is coming together," he said. "And, from all accounts, he may have been the director of your abduction attempt."

"Nice."

"In any event, the seeds of doubt have been sown. To the people in Tehran, with Mokri, it looks like they may have an Israeli agent on their hands."

"And the Iranians aren't notably forgiving to traitors."

"No, they're not," Landau agreed. "But, as a bonus, it would take out the one figure who has been blocking the rise of Hawk's agent in the hierarchy of the MOIS. If that's the case, we'll have a source there who thinks he's working for the French."

"And Mokri?"

Landau took another sip. "I think he's going to get got. They do say that revenge is sweet."

Chalice leaned back in his chair. "But didn't some Roman emperor once say something about the best revenge was to be unlike your enemy?"

Landau nodded. "I believe that would have been Marcus Aurelius. But that was then. You buy that?"

"No," Chalice smiled, raising his glass to his colleague. "Nevertheless.

Cheers."

Landau hoisted his own glass. "*Slainte.*"

= FORTY-EIGHT =

PASDARAN

Tehran, Iran
November 1, 2005

It was late afternoon. Javed Mokri's young son was playing in the yard in front of their Elahiyeh home under the watchful gaze of the nanny. The boy was cheerfully and repeatedly kicking a soccer ball against the stone wall of the yard. Until something from his peripheral vision caught his attention.

The boy had, of course, seen military vehicles in the streets of Tehran before, but never in his own neighborhood.

The nanny pulled him aside protectively as three SUVs with tan and brown camouflage coloring came to a stop at the front gate. At once, all of the doors swung open, allowing several grim-faced men to exit the vehicles.

The boy abruptly stopped at his play "What is happening *Dayeh*?" he asked.

"Nothing," the nanny said, stroking his hair comfortingly. "It is nothing."

But to herself, as the men entered the yard, she whispered "*Pasdaran*."

The IRGC had come to call.

* * *

Javed was again in his study when the door was pushed open and the uniformed Pasdaran men entered the room uninvited. He looked up in alarm. "What is this?" he demanded. "Why are you intruding into my home?"

The senior officer bowed his head and placed a hand over his heart. "*Jenab*," he said. Excellency. "My superiors have asked to see you."

"When?"

"Now, *Jenab*."

Mokri shook his head. "This is not proper," he sputtered.

The officer remained mute.

"And if I were to refuse this request?"

"I am sorry, but you may not refuse," the officer said. "Now, please stand up and come with us."

When Mokri hesitated, two of the other IRGC men moved in, forcibly extracting him from his chair and cuffing his hands behind his back.Mokri's son and the nanny watched in horror as Mokri was taken out of the home and placed in one of the SUVs.

Neither could grasp the significance of what had just transpired.

= FORTY-NINE =

EVIN PRISON

Tehran, Iran
December 10, 2005

Built in 1972 in the hills northwest of Tehran, Evin Prison was designed to hold the enemies of the Shah. After the revolution, the Islamic regime expanded the facility from a 300 to 1,500 prisoner capacity. The prison continued on its mission, merely shifting the ideology of its occupants.

On November 7th, a Special Revolutionary Court was convened within the confines of Evin Prison. The accused was Javed Mokri.

Following his arrest Mokri was housed in a plain cell in Section 209 of the prison. Appropriately enough, Section 209 was under the direct control of the MOIS.

After nearly a month of confinement, Mokri was led into a small conference hall that was being used as a courtroom. A senior judge and four secondary judges were awaiting him. As was the prosecutor and his defense attorney.

The trial was conducted swiftly. Mokri was charged with four violations of the Iranian Penal Code. The charges included violations of:

*Article 501 - Crimes against the national security of the Iranian state;

*Article 502 - Espionage.

*Article 505 - Gathering sensitive information under the cover of state

authority.

*Article 508 - Cooperation with foreign states against the interest of the

Islamic Republic.

The prosecutor spent roughly an hour presenting the evidence against Mokri. Evidence that had largely been supplied via the influence of Shahriar Parviz.

The defense attorney made his case in less than thirty minutes. It was premised upon Mokri's long service on behalf of the Revolution, his long service to the security aims of the Islamic Republic, and his close and proven ties to the Supreme National Security Council and to Hassan Rouhani himself.

The prosecutor quickly leapt upon the final point, charging that his traitorous actions despite those same close, high-level ties made him an especially heinous criminal.

The court then adjourned to deliberate.

Forty-five minutes later, the court returned. The chief judge ordered Mokri to stand to hear the decision of the court. The news was not unexpected.

As to the violation of Article 501: guilty.

As to the violation of Article 502: guilty.

As to the violation of Article 505: guilty.

And, as to the violation of Article 508: guilty.

The sentence was death. By hanging.

* * *

Javed Mokri sat in his solitary cell for another two days. He was given the opportunity to meet with members of his family, but he declined the offer. Better not to increase their suffering by seeing him in this condition.

In the early hours of the appointed morning, a pair of guards entered Mokri's cell. There was no reason to awaken him. He was waiting for them.

The guards ordered him to stand up. Complying, Mokri's hands were then secured tightly behind his back. That task completed, he was taken out of his cell and led to a small, open-air courtyard.

It was 0400 hours, well before the call to morning prayer. A faint glitter of stars still shone in the sky above.

Mokri immediately took note of the fact that a makeshift wooden gallows had been erected in the corner of the yard. The structure was not unfamiliar to him. Not at all.

It was illuminated by a garish floodlight. A photographer with a video camera was standing by, as was a small delegation of witnesses and officials.

A single strand of a blue plastic rope dangled from the crossbar of the gallows. At the end of the rope was a thick, coarse noose.

Mokri paused momentarily to absorb the sight awaiting him. Finally nodding to the assembled personages, he slowly mounted the steps of the gallows. He stood mute and emotionless as the noose was affixed about his neck and the presiding official began to read the charges and the death warrant. He wasn't paying attention. He could only appreciate the irony of the situation.

Mokri had been a witness, if not the cause, of many similar executions many times throughout his career. Never had he imagined that he would once be falsely accused of criminal actions and find himself on the other end of revolutionary justice.

The rituals concluded, the presiding official nodded to one of the guards who unceremoniously yanked the support out from under the plank on which Mokri was standing.

The executioner's rope had no slack. Consequently, there was no neck-breaking drop. Mokri, like so many before him, and so many to follow him, was left to die at the end of the rope by the process of simple, and agonizing, strangulation.

As the witnesses silently watched, Mokri's legs kicked wildly, as if attempting to find purchase on some invisible perch in mid-air. To no avail.

Mercifully, within a minute, Mokri lapsed into unconsciousness and fell silent under the rope. Shortly thereafter, he was dead.

Satisfied that the sentence had been duly carried out, the presiding official waited a short bit longer and then raised a hand.

The video recording then stopped, and the floodlight was shut down. The necessary had been legally accomplished.

= FIFTY =

AND SO IT GOES

Istanbul, Turkey
February 14, 2006

February 14th. Valentine's Day. It seemed to be a fairly odd choice of dates for a clandestine meeting, but there it was.

This was Hawk's first visit to Istanbul, the premier city of the Republic of Turkey. To say that the city had a long history was to give it short shrift.

As was the case with many historic locales, the area had been initially founded by the Greeks as a colony circa 300 BC. The city progressed to become a major Byzantine power, developed as such by Constantine the Great and eventually surrounded by its massive Theodosian Walls. Constantinople survived for 1,500 years, becoming the Eastern capital of the Roman Empire until the year of 1453.

It was in 1453, after a murderous siege that lasted fifty days, that the Muslim Ottoman forces under the youthful Sultan Mehmet II finally broke through the city's defenses and conquered it. The Muslim forces subsequently overran the city, killing the ruling Byzantine emperor in the process and claiming it as their own. It was a shocking and world-changing historical event.

Despite the chill of the air, Hawk was seated on the veranda of a coffee shop awaiting the meeting. Sampling the thick coffee from his cup, Hawk took in one of the most famed views of the city: the famed Hagia Sofia Mosque.

The multi-domed structure began as a Byzantine Christian church in the first century AD and remained so for nearly a thousand years until the fall of the city. Now an Islamic Mosque and a museum, it was a famed tourist destination.

But Hawk's thoughts were less focused on the developments of the 15th century and more on the issues of the day. Specifically, why had his ostensible Iranian agent, Shahriar Parviz, requested an expedited meeting at this very location three days ago?

It had not escaped Hawk that the current JADE SORCERER case began with just such an Iranian request for a meeting in San Juan, Puerto Rico. It ended with the attempted abduction, and near death, of Chalice.

With that thought in mind, Hawk had again arranged for an armed countersurveillance team to cover and monitor the meet. The team was composed of Bear and the two trusted Bosniaks, Zlatko and Escobar.

The area had been earlier and unobtrusively electronically swept by a pair of Org technicians, with support from the US Consulate, to ensure that no listening devices had been installed.

Escobar was seated alone on the veranda, three tables away from Hawk. He was nursing a pot of sweetened tea and seemingly perusing a news magazine. In his lap was an unzipped fanny pack that concealed a silenced handgun.

As Hawk took in the scenery, the BlackBerry device on his table began to vibrate. Checking the screen, he saw that it was a message from Bear, who was situated some block or two away from the cafe.

"*DANTE here and moving,*" it said, referring to the agreed upon designation of Parviz. "*In your direction. Clear.*"

"*Okay,*" Hawk typed.

"*Agreed*," came another message, this time from Zlatko. "*Still clear. Moving. And following.*"

"Understood," Hawk replied.

Escobar and Hawk made eye contact. Got it, the latter signaled with a nearly imperceptible nod.

After several more minutes, the device again came to life. It was Bear. "*DANTE on the set. Still clear.*"

"*Agreed*," sent Zlatko. "*All clear*."

Moments later, the figure of Parviz appeared, coming up from the steps to the veranda. He was bearded and wearing sunglasses and a tweed flat cap.

Hawk rose to greet him. "My friend," he said, shaking his hand. "Very good to see you again."

"And you, Monsieur Alban, " Parviz agreed, taking a seat at the table. He removed his sunglasses and doffed his cap.

They made small talk until a waiter appeared. Zlatko and Bear hovered out of sight below the veranda.

"Coffee? Maybe tea?" Hawk offered.

Parviz shook his head dismissively. "Scotch whiskey," he said. "Two doubles. McCallan's, if you have it."

The waiter nodded and scooted off to fetch the order.

"And so," Hawk began, getting immediately to the point. "As I said, it is good to see you. But what is the reason for this unexpected meeting?"

Parviz toyed with his sunglasses. "You are, of course, aware of developments back home," he said.

"Javed," Hawk said, referring to Javed Mokri.

"Yes," the Iranian agreed. "He was, uh, removed. By the authorities. Issues with the Jews, it is said."

"Sad."

Parviz allowed himself a bit of a smirk. "Yes. Very sad for him. Rather better for me."

"How so?"

"His removal from this life also removed his multiple blockages of my advancement. I have consequently been promoted."

"My congratulations. How so?"

"European Operations," he said. "I am soon to be appointed Director of that department."

"Ah."

They paused as the waiter returned with the requested two glasses of Scotch. Thanking the waiter and dismissing him, they raised the glasses in a toast to each other.

"*A votre sante*," Hawk said.

"And to yours," Parviz agreed, taking a sip.

"And to your appointment as Director of European Operations, "Hawk continued. "That is very fortuitous. For both of us."

"It is," Parviz agreed. "But I must tell you that you have been a part of my rise as well."

Hawk waited for the reveal.

"I reported," Parviz continued, that I have successfully recruited a senior operative of the French Intelligence service."

"As in?"

"As in you, Alban," Parviz competed the thought. "This not only elevates my status at home, but it gives me additional legitimate reasons to meet with you operationally as well."

"Clever," Hawk agreed. "It opens up quite a few new possibilities for us... Well done."

Parviz took another swig of his whiskey. "And, if you will permit, the increased value should maybe be balanced with increased compensation."

Hawk paused, feigning a degree of consideration of this proposal. Finally, he nodded affirmatively. "That has merit. I will take it back to my people and get an answer for you."

"Yes," Parviz agreed. "Hopefully a generous answer."

Hawk drained his glass and set it back on the tabletop. "We will get back to you through the usual channel once we have an answer," he said.

"I look forward to it," Parviz said. "But unfortunately, my time is short so I must be on my way for now."

"Of course."

They shook hands and Parviz took his leave. As he did so, Bear and the Bosniaks drifted along in his wake to complete their surveillance of his trek.

"*Still clear,*" Bear messaged back. "*Dante, good to go.*"

"*Got it,*" Hawk typed. He peered at the BlackBerry one more time and slipped it into his pocket.

Now sitting alone on the veranda, he ordered another Scotch and took a few moments to reflect on the unexpected developments. Undoubtedly, the case was proceeding even better than had been expected. But still, it was hardly without its risks. The Iranians were not to be underestimated.

Hawk shook his head with a wry smile.

"And so it goes," he murmured to himself. "And so it goes."

=END=